The Unknown Stigma 3

3

〈The Universe〉

IRH Press

BOOKS

IRH PRESS

New York

ISBN 13: 978-1-958655-00-9

ISBN 10: 1-958655-00-7

Printed in Japan

First Edition

The Unknown Stigma

3

〈The Universe〉

Ryuho Okawa

IRH Press

1.

Earth's apocalyptic state was still shown on a large screen even as the spaceship was moving away from Earth and approaching the Moon.

Agnes thought back to the Book of Revelation. The details of the book were ambiguous, but the events unfolding in front of her very eyes were clear and specific, leaving no room for misinterpretation.

She witnessed the end of Earth's Seventh Civilization; she kept trying to save Earth to the best of her ability, but she could not even save the people close to her; she understood how Father God, the embodiment of love and mercy, is also the strict God of Judgment; and He was the One she must really call "Father"... All kinds of thoughts like this flew around in her head.

Yet, Agnes fell into deeper thought, *what exactly was the turning point for Earth's human*

Unveiling the Secret

of

The Unknown Stigma,

VISIT

https://okawabooks.com/the-unknown-stigma

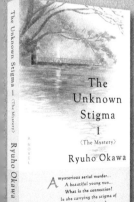

The Unknown Stigma 1 〈The Mystery〉

Ryuho Okawa

The Unknown Stigma 1 〈The Mystery〉

Ryuho Okawa

A NOVEL

A mysterious serial murder...
A beautiful young nun...
What is the connection?
Is she carrying the stigma of
light or darkness?

The Unknown Stigma 2 〈The Resurrection〉

Ryuho Okawa

The Unknown Stigma 2 〈The Resurrection〉

A NOVEL

Ryuho Okawa

A mysterious young nun with a noble mission...
What kind of destiny will unfold before her?
Will it be hope or despair?

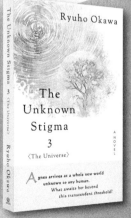

The Unknown Stigma 3 〈The Universe〉

Ryuho Okawa

The Unknown Stigma 3 〈The Universe〉

A NOVEL

Agnes arrives at a whole new world
unknown to any human.
What awaits her beyond
this transcendent threshold?

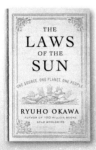

Win
a Free Book!

DISCOVER THE TRUTH
BEHIND THE MYSTERY

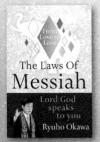

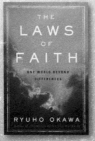

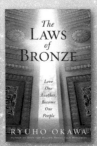

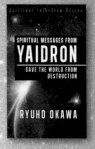

SCAN HERE TO
WIN A FREE BOOK
FROM THE
ABOVE LIST

race to either be allowed to live or be wiped out? Was there still a chance for humanity to change their future with their own will and decisions?

If Father God had forsaken humanity in the 21st century, what was the root cause of His decision?

Nuclear war—perhaps that was a part of it. But General Yaidron and the others had the technology and weapons to disable and destroy nuclear weapons. With a little push, all nuclear weapons on Earth could have been removed.

Years of colonial rule and racial discrimination—perhaps that was another factor. But that was why people were trying hard to promote human rights diplomacy and movements to overcome the North-South divide and the wealth gap between the rich and the poor.

The conflict between the communist and capitalist camps—this had a dramatic shift around 1990. The Soviet Union collapsed; the People's

Republic of China survived by liberalizing its markets and choosing a path toward modified socialism.

During the Vietnam War, the United States of America tried to protect South Vietnam, but South Vietnam lost against North Vietnam, which was backed by the Chinese Communist Party and the Soviet Union. In the end, the U.S. military retreated from Saigon in their helicopters. However, communism did not last in Vietnam, and the Vietnamese turned to a market economy and restored relations with the United States.

India, formerly a socialist country, transitioned to a liberal market economy in the 1990s and showed positive economic development. India was undergoing changes as they maintained relations with both Russia and U.S.-Japan.

Regarding inter-Korean relations, North and South Korea were long divided after World War II. Even though North Korea was a dictatorship that possessed missiles equipped with atomic or hydrogen warheads, the United Nations could have peacefully integrated the two Koreas after my "YES, U-turn" prayer against their nuclear missiles proved effective. The U.S. military alone could have deterred North Korea from becoming a nuclear superpower. Japan would have suffered millions of casualties, but that is nothing compared to the lives of eight billion people worldwide. With the power of General Yaidron and the Space Federation, North Korea shouldn't have been a problem. The only problems left were China's human rights abuses and plans to invade Hong Kong and Taiwan, but the Chinese could have been contained if the Group of Seven (G7) and the Quad (the U.S., Japan, Australia, and India) had worked together to impose economic sanctions and use military force.

Or was Lord God angered by Earth's contamination with the coronavirus that had originated in Wuhan, China, and its hidden nature as a weapon for global warfare? But the coronavirus pandemic was starting to make its way back to China, and it was anticipated that the pandemic would end in five years or so.

If that was not the cause, could the Russo–Ukrainian War have led to the extinction of humankind? With effective economic sanctions against Russia as well as enough monetary funds and provisions of weapons, ammunition, and food to Ukraine from Western countries and Japan, Russian forces could have withdrawn. An all-out nuclear war could have happened in the next stage. Where did things go wrong?

Perhaps Lord God viewed the conflict between Islamic fundamentalism and Israel as irredeemable. The religious conflict involving Christianity had been going on for well over a millennium, and certainly, long-lasting strife was anticipated to continue.

Or did humankind make mistakes about the issues of climate change and renewable energy? But they would have found out the truth by around 2050.

Or did God react—as He did in the story of Sodom and Gomorrah—against the LGBTQ movement that Obamiden and others tried to push forth and create a Noah's Ark-like catastrophe?

If not, did God view "neo-social welfarism," a variation of democracy, to be creating a society worse than communism? Under communism, those who do not work are sent to jail; under the neo-social welfare system, the government simply gives away money to those who do not work and keeps on building up budget deficits.

And the final question is regarding the Earth invasion plan by malicious aliens. Which countries, and which leaders, did these malicious aliens infiltrate? It was probably impossible for the eight billion people on Earth and even international organizations such as the United Nations and the International Court of Justice to determine that.

Two most recent U.S. presidents announced the existence of unidentified flying objects, but even developed countries around the world lagged behind in obtaining information on them. The topic was handled only by niche television programs—nothing more.

In fact, I am currently on board the flagship, Andromeda Galaxy, *but the people on Earth cannot fathom the existence of such a spacecraft.*

Materialism driven by "almighty science" came to be the core of academia and mass media, but unexpectedly, Earth's science was still far too primitive for a space age. Perhaps Lord God was angered because "science" had fused with materialism to persecute "faith."

The dark side of the Moon would come in sight in no time.

Agnes must carefully remember what would happen from now on. All for when she would come back to Earth again…

2.

The Moon appeared larger and larger. Agnes started seeing countless craters. There was no air. Thus, there was no oxygen. Agnes wondered whether a place like this could sustain life.

There were various theories about the Moon's formation. Some said the Moon came to be when Earth's Pacific region broke off, whereas others said meteorites were attracted by Earth's gravitational pull and accreted to form the Moon. But an analysis of the composition of a rock from the Moon showed the rock to be as old as Earth, which was said to have been formed 4.6 billion years ago. Surely, no one would believe in the Japanese folklore of a rabbit pounding mochi on the Moon, but some kind of food, along with water, air, and a suitable temperature, would be necessary for life to be born.

The Japanese tale of Princess Kaguya was born more than 1,300 years ago, but the more you read the story, the more it feels like the princess was an alien. An old bamboo cutter finds a shining bamboo in a bamboo grove, and he sees a tiny girl in the bamboo. If Agnes remembered correctly, the bamboo cutter finds gold coins along with the girl. The tiny girl grows to become a beautiful lady in about three months.

Then, the princess is proposed to by nobles from the capital, but she makes them give up by presenting completely unreasonable demands.

In the meantime, she tells the old bamboo cutter that she must return to the Moon on the night of a full moon. Armed soldiers guard the garden and the rooftop with bows and arrows, and surely, the Moon's army comes flying on the clouds. The heavenly beings, with Shakyamuni Buddha at the center, come to pick up Princess Kaguya while playing music. Soldiers armed with bows and arrows are unable to move at all, bound by an invisible force. Princess Kaguya is lifted up through the air into an oxcart and returns to Moon world. That was the gist of the story. Agnes thought that the story was too similar to a UFO report to be read as an ancient novel.

First and foremost, the tiny girl shining inside the bamboo can be read as a tiny spaceship and a tiny alien. Many UFOs glow at night. There are also numerous reports of women on Earth being abducted into UFOs, having children with aliens, and these children growing to become adults in several months.

It is also commonly said that airplane instruments stopped working when UFOs appeared or that when people encountered aliens, they could not move their bodies, as if they had sleep paralysis. Perhaps the tale of Princess Kaguya is based on true experiences rather than on imagination.

It is also interesting that Shakyamuni Buddha came riding on a cloud to pick her up.

The tale of Princess Kaguya didn't make a clear distinction between the universe and heaven of the Spirit World, but Agnes knew that her Heavenly Father was connected to Shakyamuni Buddha.

Maybe I'm now going through something similar to what Princess Kaguya went through, Agnes thought.

Agnes also found the tale of Urashima Taro intriguing. Taro the fisherman rescues a turtle, which then invites him to the Realm of Dragon Gods; he spends three years there having fun, but when he returns to his village, 300 years have already passed. The Dragon Palace could have been on a "water planet" in another part of the universe, and what felt like three years could have been 300 years in a world beyond the speed of light, and vice versa.

General Yaidron said he was supporting Moses from his UFO when Moses left Egypt more than 3,000 years ago. So Agnes was not sure about his actual age.

In fact, Father God, El Cantare, could be over 100 billion years old. When Agnes started thinking deeply about it, her head went spinning.

"You'll find out soon," said a 4-foot guide robot that looked like a Japanese beauty. It continued:

"The Moon contains some underground cavities, and although small, there are underground cities. There are artificial, self-circulating rivers and artificial lighting that is as bright as the lighting inside Tokyo Dome. There are small pet animals and vegetable gardens. There are also insects, and new creature species are being studied. Some space people have been living on the Moon ever since they arrived here at some point during Earth's past civilizations. There are dozens of alien species living mainly on the dark side of the

Moon that cannot be seen from Earth. It serves as their base from which to go for Earth's missions. But not all of them are allies; some of them are hostile forces."

"What kind of space people are they?" Agnes asked the guide robot.

"Take a look at the monitor. Do you see the structure that looks like a giant mussel? The Reptilians who do evil on Earth still live there. This time around, they were deeply involved in China and North Korea."

"So, what will Father do?"

At that moment, three main cannons came out of the front deck of *Andromeda Galaxy*'s streamlined hull.

The three cannons turned 45 degrees to the left and fired beams of light.

The giant-mussel-shaped enemy base closed its mouth opening and tried to retreat underground.

Next, four missiles were fired from the rear of the flagship. The mussel-shaped defense base was destroyed, and several aliens with insect faces, like the Japanese TV superhero, *Kamen Rider*, fled out of the base. They escaped on motorcycle-like vehicles in all directions across the surface of the Moon.

About 10 small UFOs, each about 30 feet in diameter, took off from the flagship and destroyed the fleeing aliens one after another with laser beam guns.

"What goes around comes around. We are now cleaning up the evil they were doing on Earth," Father God spoke.

The Lord said, "They have been chipping away at the faith of Earthlings in return for sharing some of their scientific technology."

"Is everything done?" Agnes asked.

"General Yaidron is supposed to take down the enemy general, Bazooka, who is in an underground base. It's that 100-foot UFO that is about to escape from the Moon."

Mr. Yaidron's battleship destroyed Bazooka's spacecraft with its whirling laser beam cannon.

It was Agnes' first time witnessing a real space war.

3.

Agnes understood that the Moon's alien base functioned as a place to gather information about Earth and that it was a place for space beings who had left Earth's sphere to rest before moving to other planets.

"How many space beings live on the Moon?" Agnes asked the guide robot.

"Well, usually two to three thousand space beings, but sometimes it can be in the tens of thousands before a major event or after the arrival of a UFO mother ship."

"Where in the world are the entrance and the exit?"

"Please take a close look at the monitor. Do you see the hemispherical, transparent dome above that large crater there? Once that thing opens, there will be a large hole in the crater area for spaceships to go in and out."

"I wonder if Father will stay on the Moon for a few nights."

"This time, the enemy's main force is fleeing to Mars, so the battle will most likely continue in pursuit of them."

"But I'd like to walk on the Moon at least once. I guess America stopped sending people to the Moon after the Apollo program because they encountered UFOs, a UFO base, and aliens, and they felt it dangerous. If I walk on the Moon's surface, maybe someone will come to watch."

"My goodness, Ms. Agnes, how fearless you are! You'll surely feel like a rabbit if you walk on the Moon."

Thus, Agnes decided to take a walk on the Moon. The limit was 15 minutes. Once she put on a space suit and landed on the ground, her body felt light.

"Hop, step, jump!"

Take one step, and she could jump as far

as 15–30 feet. *This is fun.* She saw a scorpion-looking creature coming out from under a rock.

She remotely heard the voice of her guide robot.

"The scorpion is a machine for surveillance. A watchman of an underground city is observing you through the eyes of the scorpion. Please don't break it."

Upon hearing that, Agnes felt like playing a prank.

She bent down a little and picked up a handy lump of rock. "Hey!" She threw it toward the scorpion-shaped robot. The rock felt light. Or rather, it flew 100 feet. The scorpion panicked and crawled underground. Even though it was just a robot, it seemed to protect itself like any other living creature.

Some dust flew up whenever she jumped. But there was no wind. Agnes looked up and saw countless stars twinkling above. Then, three UFOs came into view on the horizon.

I have to get back soon.

The moment Agnes had the thought, she was sucked into the flagship by a powerful magnetic beam. She found herself back in her seat wearing a pink outfit with an *RO* mark.

"Father, wasn't the story of the Moon rabbit, after all, about a person who actually walked on the Moon in the past? How else would Earthlings know that you can walk on the surface of the Moon as if you are hopping around?"

"That's right. Even in past civilizations, there were humans who came to the Moon. There were also those who went to Earth and talked to Earthlings about weightlessness on the Moon. Maybe that's why the rabbit often comes up in the story of the Moon," the Lord said.

He continued.

"Now, then, let's go to Mars. The Moon is about one-quarter the size of Earth, but Mars is about one-half the size of Earth. There used to be rivers flowing on the surface of Mars and there was air, but it became the stage for a space war a long time ago. Now, Mars has poor living conditions. There are ice caps the size of Earth's Greenland at the northern and southern poles, and there is water underground. The planet looks red because there are many iron oxides on its surface, some of which are used for making spacecraft. There is a thin atmosphere composed of carbon dioxide, but space beings have built a large underground city. Our base is near a great canyon called the Marina Valley that is 25 miles wide and nearly 2,500 miles long."

After Father God said so, Agnes' ship arrived in the sky over Mars in about 15 minutes. Apparently, the areas exposed to the Sun had a very high temperature, and the areas not exposed to the Sun were extremely cold. Thus, most aliens had bases slightly larger than those on the Moon in Mars' underground city. The city was said to have artificial ceilings and artificial lighting. Native Martians looked like tall chickens, and they were highly intelligent. They were said to be utilizing many Grey-type cyborgs to do various work. Some cyborgs were said to be using the brains of humans who were once brought over from Earth. These humans were now an extinct race.

Agnes noticed that Yaidron and his UFO fleet were also following them to Mars. It must mean that there would be another battle to be fought here.

As they were about to land on the right side of the Marina Valley, dozens of transparent domes opened up. Once the battleships got inside, the domes automatically closed. Then, what appeared to be the surface of Mars split wide open, leading the flagship, *Andromeda Galaxy*, and other UFOs to an underground airport.

They got off the ship and entered a building near the control tower. All kinds of space beings were walking around the hallways—just like in the movie *Men in Black*.

Agnes obtained more information from Father God. The aliens seemed to be working for the Space Federation's Earth task force.

She heard various names, including Vega, Deneb, Sirius, Altair, Centaurus, Ursa Minor, Cassiopeia, Andromeda, and Sagittarius.

Agnes would not be able to understand everything immediately. But she understood that the volunteers from these stars and constellations were apparently protecting the solar system—and Earth, especially.

Aliens also seemed to be living on Jupiter's satellite, Europa.

"We are going to war tomorrow," Father's voice echoed.

4.

Dawn broke over the underground city on Mars. In fact, the city had an artificial sun, so the day progressed according to the color shift of its light: pale indigo light shone during the nighttime, the light beam became slightly orange at dawn, and during the daytime, it became the color of the midday Sun. Apparently, the light would turn back to orange in the evening. Agnes looked at the clock and saw that it was 6:30 a.m. She would have to leave at 8:00 a.m., so she had to get ready quickly. While Agnes was taking a shower, a spherical television appeared out of the wall and streamed three different news reports at once. Somehow, she was able to understand all three reports at the same time.

She watched the news about Mars while she showered for about 10 minutes. The news included occasional reports of Earth and other planets.

The dryer made no sound, and she was able to dry everything from her hair to her entire body in one minute. The toilet was of great wonder. Something like an octopus' sucker stuck onto the butt, and after three signals, *tap-tap-tap*, feces and urine were sucked up, followed by 15 seconds of washing and drying the butt.

Clothing was organized as indoor and outdoor clothes, and upon entering the respective box, a person was automatically dressed. In addition, the indoor clothes were fluffy like loungewear. That morning, Agnes chose the color white.

Agnes' room was about 170 square feet in size. Her breakfast was served on a table that rose from the floor. A 4-foot-tall waitress robot came out with the table to serve her.

Just as Agnes thought of opening the curtains, a window appeared out of the blue. She seemed to be in a room of a tower hotel.

The view out the window was somewhat like New York; there was a flowing river that looked like the Hudson River, and there also stood the Empire State Building and the twin towers of the World Trade Center that had collapsed on September 11, 2001, on Planet Earth. The waitress robot chatted that the twin towers had been recreated after Lord El Cantare's fond memories of them.

Breakfast consisted of soup, bread, artificial meat, fruits, and café au lait. Of course, she was able to change her order based on her physical condition on that day.

During the meal, she watched a Mars guide that was playing on a screen on the wall. The "Space Federation" or the "Interplanetary Alliance" had an underground city with a population of one million along the great canyon. The whole city seemed to be a United-Nations-like-place of the solar system.

On the other hand, the malicious aliens who had been eating away at Earth's civilization over several millennia seemed to have a hideout below the ice cap at the northern pole. They also seemed to have built a hierarchical organization, and it was said that the organization consisted of space species that had a strong desire for destruction and lacked love and harmony, along with people who had been expelled from past civilizations on Earth. The total membership was said to be 20,000–30,000, but because these malicious aliens were skilled in "walking-into" Earth's authority figures by using them like their avatars, they had induced rebellions and corruption all over Earth. Moreover, they had battleships, cruisers, and a fleet of UFOs. Bazooka's UFO that was destroyed on the Moon was said to have largely influenced Earth's recent turmoil.

Now, 10 minutes before 8:00 a.m., a guide robot came over and led Agnes to the flagship,

Andromeda Galaxy. They descended via a transparent elevator to the passageway leading to the ship's entrance.

Agnes was given a brief tour of the inside of the ship. The battleship was over 2,600 feet in length and 650 feet in width, but she was told that the ship would morph into a different shape depending on the type of battle.

Today, the entire space fleet—about 1,000 ships in total—was going to be mobilized. The ships that needed to be repaired were fixed up throughout the night.

The guide robot told her that 200 aliens and about 300 robots were on board *Galaxy*. Agnes was told that the details would be explained later and that for today, she just needed to remain in the control tower and observe the battle. The commander-in-chief was Lord God, but in practice, a space being known as Commander Z was captain of the ship. Agnes was told that his true identity would be revealed to her once the battle was over.

It was now 8:00 a.m. There was a signal that sounded like *Phweeeen!* and a hatch on the surface of Mars opened, followed by the opening of the semicircular dome.

A large army of a total of 1,000 spacecraft gathered approximately 1,600 feet above the Marina Valley.

Father God gave a brief greeting and ordered the army to not let Ahriman, the main perpetrator of the collapse of Earth's Seventh Civilization, escape.

All spaceships headed toward the sky above the northern pole on Mars. The tip of an iceberg opened up and a tunnel appeared.

Enemy UFOs gushed out one after another.

The main players seemed to be the ships of Yaidron and R. A. Goal. *How will this decisive battle on Mars play out?* Agnes wondered and turned to Father God to her right to read His facial expression.

Father stayed silent, however.

It was the start of a brand-new experience.

5.

The ice cap on the northern pole of Mars was about the size of Greenland. If there was an underground base here, it would not be easy to destroy the enemy's entire force. The allied forces must lure the enemy general to come out.

Now, about 100 small UFOs flew out in front of Agnes. Most of them were single-seater UFOs with Grey aliens, probably for the purpose of scouting out the allied forces. If the Grey aliens saw that there was no chance of winning, they would choose a strategy to hole up under the ice cap. That was how they had always survived in the past.

Nevertheless, this time, Lord God was on the side of the allied forces, and the flagship, *Andromeda Galaxy*, was making its first appearance. The allied forces would have to achieve brilliant results in the battle. The true intention of Lord

God would be to strike a blow against not only Ahriman but also Kandahar, the commander-in-chief of the evil gods, who was involved in ruling the entire dark-side universe.

First, an aerial battle took place among the small UFOs. The battle was overwhelmingly in favor of the allied forces because they fought with 300 spaceships against 100 enemy ships.

Even though the allied forces had the upper hand, it was hard to see the enemies who used a chameleon tactic, emitting the color of ice on the outside and blending with icebergs in the background.

The enemy force used cyborgs called Grey, so the allied forces struggled with reading their minds like they could do against humans.

The allied forces' left-wing battleship, *Enlightenment 1*, was headed by R. A. Goal. R. A. Goal went beyond the enemy fleet of small UFOs and fired a green light beam from the top of the iceberg. Now, the iceberg looked like a green mountain. The enemy UFOs were still shimmering silver, so they were easily targeted and locked on by the allied forces' small flying saucers. The allied forces shot light beams and fired missiles. Many enemy spacecraft were shot down.

Next, three Manta-ray-like cruisers, each about 330 feet long, flew out of the hole in the iceberg. These cruisers were probably equipped with missiles and laser beam cannons. Seven or eight small ally UFOs were shot down. The light beam from ally UFOs seemed to have caused some damage, but they weren't powerful enough to shoot the cruisers down. The right-wing battleship of Yaidron went forth. Yaidron's ship was a large UFO over 650 feet in diameter; Yaidron was a professional fighter, so the enemy force was startled upon seeing the letter "*Y*" on the back of Yaidron's flying saucer.

Yaidron launched something like light rings, about 25 feet in diameter, from each side of his battleship. It was a new weapon. The light rings rapidly spun like ninja stars, or throwing knives, slicing two of the three enemy cruisers in half. Then, the rings hit the ice cap and kept zipping forward, cutting through as far as several hundreds of feet of ice. If there was a hollow inside, along with an enemy base, much of it should have been utterly destroyed. Indeed, fire and smoke were spewing from all over the iceberg.

Galaxy's three main cannons fired laser beams at the remaining cruiser and destroyed it.

At last, the enemy force mobilized the battleship, *All Black*, which was also their flagship that carried Ahriman. It was escorted by 10 UFOs that were about 160 feet in length.

The main cannon of the enemy battleship fired a rainbow beam and destroyed an ally's cruiser,

Old Goat. This ship carried a goat-like alien named "Peaceful Mind," a diplomat who had followed the allied forces from their Moon base. He was able to speak 100 different space languages; alas, he fell to the reddish-brown surface of Mars upon being hit by the enemy's cannon. Surely, his rescue team would come for him from the base.

One by one, the enemy's 10 escort ships shot down small UFOs of the allies.

From the allied forces, a triangular, black cruiser called *Eagle Mind* swooped down from the sky. *Eagle Mind* carried a total of eight missiles, four on each wing. The missiles had a system to track down the enemy wherever they went once the target was locked on.

Five enemy escort ships were driven out of combat. Two ships fled into the iceberg tunnel, but a major explosion occurred inside the tunnel.

The other three escort ships were blasted by three gigantic missiles that were launched from the front tip of the flagship, *Galaxy*.

As Agnes wondered what Ahriman would do next, his ship, *All Black*, began to flee into outer space.

Yaidron's ship went after it. Ahriman was trying to escape from Mars toward Jupiter.

Ahriman was scared of the letter "Y" printed on Yaidron's ship. Many of his spacecraft had been shot down by this single ship. The official name of Yaidron's ship was *God Fire*. *God Fire* launched a net-shaped light beam from its main cannon. Ahriman's battleship was caught by a net of light. This net of light was attached to the main cannon of Yaidron's ship by a rope composed of light.

Yaidron's spacecraft pulled Ahriman's battleship back to the skies above Mars with great force, capturing the enemy alive.

Ahriman's battleship was brought in front of the Lord God.

If *Galaxy* shot its main cannon, Ahriman and *All Black* would be turned to dust.

Ahriman raised a white flag.

The battle of the spaceships ended in the Lord's great victory. All that remained was to arrest, confine, and interrogate Ahriman at the base on Mars and record his past wrongdoings in the cosmic record. The Lord God entrusted Yaidron to carry out these tasks.

Captain Commander Z of *Andromeda Galaxy* fired the "Final Missile Z"—10 times more destructive than a hydrogen bomb—into the center of Mars' ice cap at the northern pole. The missile rotated like a drill; it penetrated the center of the ice cap and made a massive explosion. Still, they needed to get Ahriman to confess whether Commander-in-Chief Kandahar was inside.

6.

Ahriman and Yaidron were facing each other in the interrogation room. Ahriman was about 6′3″ in height, and he was in a black outfit. The antenna-like horns on his head bent outward at one-third of their length from the tips, so if *Baikinman* from a Japanese anime had a father, he would look like this. Ahriman wore a silver belt around his waist. His physique was similar to that of a slightly slender Superman.

Sitting across a 7-foot-wide and 5-foot-long desk was Yaidron, who looked like Superman and Captain America combined. He was 7 feet tall, and he seemed to weigh about 260 pounds. An *RO* mark was engraved on the chest of his blue outfit. The belt around his waist was made of special alloys that were soft, and the belt seemed to have a multi-purpose machine built into it. He had five fingers on each hand, and his claws were

41

retractable and could be adjusted to be either long or short at his will. He wore a helmet on his head that was similar to what Captain America wore, except Yaidron had two golden horns that were each about 4 inches long. They were probably used as both weapons and communication devices.

It was extremely rare for a *Yaidron-class* general to conduct an interrogation, but because Ahriman had psychic powers and could control other people's minds, there needed to be someone who had enough power to hold down Ahriman's power—otherwise, it would be dangerous.

There were three security robots in the 530-square-feet room, but no human beings or space people with a mind were allowed in the room because they could be manipulated by Ahriman.

El Cantare, Agnes, and Yaidron's wife in space, Namiel, were watching from across the monitor. Ms. Namiel was a cosmic diva with an electric lightning bolt; she had inspired songs such as *The Real Exorcist.*

"So you are Ahriman, the archenemy from the time of Zoroaster's descent. Is that correct?" Yaidron asked.

"Yes. I am also the god of darkness," Ahriman said.

"What kind of work have you done recently?"

"I gave Jesus Christ the last temptation when he was on the cross."

"Give me the specifics."

"I told him, 'God has abandoned you. Curse God. Tell people that you are not God's only son, beg for your life, and marry Mary Magdalene to build a happy family.'"

"What else have you done?"

"I suppressed the Gnostics of Christian mysticism and crushed them as heresy. I manipulated the Christian church. And that Manichaeism, with its duality of good and evil that hinted at the return of Zoroastrianism—I mobilized Zoroastrians and Christians and sentenced Mani to death by skinning him alive."

"So that is how Manichaeism perished, huh. What next?"

"I encouraged Muhammad of Islam to practice polygamy and destroy idols and statues. That's how I shook both Christianity and Buddhism."

"What did you do after that?"

"In Japan, I led the assassination of Prince Shotoku's entire family. The next thing I didn't do alone, but during the Tang Dynasty of China, I lured Emperor Xuanzong into questioning his Buddhist faith. I also transformed Confucianism into a revolutionary ideology."

"How about the revolutions in Europe?"

"During the French Revolution, I put the king and others on the guillotine one after another. I turned the revolution into an armed communistic uprising."

"How about England?"

"I created the Church of England so that earthly powers would outmatch the pope's authority."

"What about America?"

"I guided the assassinations of Lincoln and Kennedy. Way before that, in Rome, I assassinated Caesar."

"How about the Soviet Union and Russia?"

"I entered Tolstoy's wife's mind and made her go insane. I made her fire a gun to compel Tolstoy to run away from home and die at a local train station building in solitude. There was a social movement that arose based on his philosophical and religious views, and I prevented it from becoming a religion, too."

"Tolstoy depicted Napoleon as an 'antichrist' in *War and Peace*. Did you whisper anything to him?"

"You see, I don't like the kind of society that Napoleon advocated—freedom and equality, diligence, hard work, and intelligence. It's easier for us to enter people under the imperial system. I hate a society based on hard work and competence. I also entered Lenin, Stalin, and Khrushchev, but I couldn't enter Gorbachev. Putin started the Russo–Ukrainian War. If he had given up his faith, I'm sure I could've entered him too."

"How about Germany?"

"I messed with Marx but not with Hitler. Actually, Hitler was mainly guided by an ancient Celtic god—now, a devil—who was crushed by Christianity. See, I am the one who saved Planet Earth by forcing Stalin and Franklin Roosevelt to take part in the war."

"Did you have anything to do with Mao Zedong?"

"I am busy, so I left him in the hands of my colleague, the First Emperor of Qin. But I did give him advice."

"What about Japan during and after World War II?"

"Japan is made of *tengu* (long-nosed goblins) and their downfall. Japanese Shinto's monism of light is different from the god of light, Ahura Mazda. But I was able to enter F. Roosevelt because of Japan's attack on Pearl Harbor. The one who entered Bush, the father, during the Gulf War, and the son, during the Iraq War, is an evil god related to Enlil. He is the invader from Planet Zeta, and he is your enemy."

"Any last words?"

"I like the mass media that keeps repeating, 'There is no just war.' It's Beelzebub who is mainly in charge of the media. It cancels out good and evil, making it impossible for humans to distinguish between God and the devil."

And thus, it became quite clear what Ahriman had done. Of course, he must have had companions—.

7.

According to Ahriman, Commander-in-Chief Kandahar escaped somewhere into the dark-side universe via a different route when Ahriman came out in his battleship. Unfortunately, Yaidron and the others were unable to capture one of the enemy leaders.

Agnes spoke with Namiel, General Yaidron's wife, inside a little coffee shop within the base. Namiel was about 5′7″ in height, and she looked very much like Namie Amuro, a Japanese singer from Okinawa who retired at the age of 40. Namiel turned out to be the singer's cosmic soul sister. She was apparently sending out electrifying light beams from the universe onto Namie Amuro's fans, dubbed "Amurers," during many concerts held in dome stadiums. Come to think of it, Namie wore two horn-like buns on her head;

likewise, Namiel had two round horns without sharp tips. Namiel told Agnes that she had the ability to emit electrifying light beams to excite a large crowd of people. Besides that, Namiel had other jobs, such as starting new fashion trends on Earth. She gained new ideas from cosmic fashion that Earthlings hadn't yet seen.

Agnes drank caffe latte, while Namiel drank Okinawan coffee.

"What did you think of Ahriman?" Agnes asked Namiel.

"He's a really evil one. He has done 10 times worse than what he claims he did, I'm sure," Namiel answered.

"I wonder if there's really such thing as a 'god of darkness.'"

"I bet he was interfering with the God of the Earth's plan out of jealousy. He must've been defeated on other planets, too."

"Anyhow, why is your husband Yaidron so strong?"

"I might sound like I'm boasting, but El Cantare is invincible as long as Yaidron is around. Yaidron is strong because he knows there is evil in the universe that must be destroyed and because he knows that this evil is negatively influencing Earth. However, Earthlings, for all their talk about peace and more peace, don't seem to understand 'Justice.'"

"That means they lack wisdom, huh."

"For both Earthlings and space people alike, the three-dimensional space is all about battling your temptations. But the reality is, you can't be an angel or a god of a higher dimension without a ladder called 'Faith.' I mean, Earthlings don't know that space travel is difficult unless you integrate faith and science."

"You are talking about an interdimensional warp tunnel, right?"

"There are spatial warp tunnels, and there are time warp tunnels. It seems that the Seventh Civilization on Earth, this time around, didn't reach that point."

"What do you mean?"

"It means that once you attain real enlightenment of the universe, you'll be able to transcend time and travel among different galaxies. You can also travel freely to past civilizations as well as to future civilizations."

"That's incredible. I guess Father couldn't preach that on Earth this time."

"As long as you attach yourself to worldly status, fame, financial assets, power, food, and sex, among others, you cannot transcend time, space, or civilizations."

"Did you train somewhere to master this?"

"For now, that's a secret. But you should be taught by Lord God El Cantare first. Isn't that the purpose of this space travel?"

"Oh, that's right! I forgot that Father had invited me to dinner."

Agnes said goodbye to Namiel, seeing her off with an eye of admiration.

"Great mission and great enlightenment are connected. I have more to learn."

Agnes rushed over to a restaurant called *Beautiful Garden*. El Cantare was waiting for her with a delighted smile.

"My daughter, have you made any progress in your studies?" the Lord asked.

"Yes, but only a little," Agnes responded.

"Namiel also controls lightning bolts, so she is Yaidron's right arm."

"So it was true that those with real power can attract real popularity."

"Soon, I must endow you with the enlightenment that will allow you to warp through space."

"Do I need to visualize a cosmic map in my mind?"

"My daughter, did you see any cockpit, fuel, or engine on *Andromeda Galaxy*?"

"Come to think of it, it didn't look like an ordinary rocket."

"In fact, there is no machinery of any kind. Every single thing was materialized out of spiritual energy. That is why there is no steering wheel, accelerator, or brakes. No oil, coal, or natural gas either. There is not even an engine."

The Lord continued.

"Simply put, the battleship was made by manifesting our thoughts. So you see, space travel is not about iron ships and machines flying around. What you *believe* to exist as an object is broken down into molecules, atoms, photons, and spiritons, and they travel instantaneously to the destination you have in your mind. There, the object is restored to its original form."

Just then, a waitress robot came in and served a dish that looked like steak.

Agnes chuckled.

"Then, really, this steak could also be turned into smoke," she commented.

"When you watch TV, for instance, it feels as if the characters really exist, right? It's the same with food."

"I understand. As the saying goes, 'Matter is void—void is matter.' It's about understanding Buddhism's Heart Sutra in the context of the universe, right? Things that don't exist seem to *be*, and *being* is actually an illusion. So if I can attain this level of enlightenment, I'll be able to teleport among different planets."

"It is a little early, but tomorrow, we will leave for the Andromeda Galaxy. Believe in me and follow me."

8.

I wonder what the Andromeda Galaxy is like.

Agnes was so excited that she could not sleep much. Eventually, dawn broke, and morning came. Well, she had no idea what day of the year or day of the week it was. What she thought was a one-day battle could've been much longer than that.

Anyway, it was Agnes' last morning spent on Mars. Yaidron and his wife came to see her off. Yaidron was not able to go with her to the Andromeda Galaxy because he still needed to patrol the solar system.

"Ms. Agnes," Yaidron said. "In the solar system, humans used to live on Venus, but a volcanic explosion and subsequent high-temperature sulfuric acid gas added great pressure to the planet, making it uninhabitable. The Venusian Spirit World and space station are still there, though. One of Jupiter's satellites, Europa, is inhabited by some space people who look like sea lions walking upright, and over there, the world is filled with ice and water. M31 in the Andromeda Galaxy is 2.3 million light-years away, but it's one of our home grounds. I'm sure you'll learn a lot."

"You said 2.3 million light-years? How far away is that?" Agnes asked.

"It means, flying at the speed of light would take 2.3 million years," Namiel chimed in. "In other words, you'll be a wrinkly, 2.3-million-year-old grandma by the time you arrive."

"No way! I don't want that," Agnes said.

"Einstein said that there was no speed beyond light, but you can't travel to different universes without exceeding the speed of light. Ask the Father God," Namiel said.

Thus, Agnes boarded *Andromeda Galaxy* as several people saw her off.

"If it takes 2.3 million years at the speed of light, will we be going to the future? Or the past?

I wonder if Earth will be back in the primitive age the next time I return to Earth. Or maybe I'll arrive at the end of the Eighth Civilization."

As Agnes mumbled under her breath, the Lord spoke: "Just believe. The Great Universe was created by God. The Universe is God's garden."

"Now, let us depart," the Lord said.

"So, who is that captain, Commander Z?" Agnes asked.

"He is the cosmic form of God Hermes. You will soon find out what the sandals of Hermes truly mean."

Vrooom. It was time to depart. Space started to become distorted. To Agnes, the ship was like a whale that was passing through a tunnel of an infinitely extending mirror. She felt as if her height was alternatively growing and shrinking to a large extent. Then, her body was broken down into countless molecules, which were further broken down into atoms, protons, photons, and spiritons. *So this is the so-called warp*, Agnes thought. She could no longer see her body, but she still existed as a thinking being. She heard words from somewhere: *In the beginning was thought. Thought created matter*. It must be the words of the Lord.

Agnes heard a *Phweeeen*, and she felt the ship slow down. It was as if they were coming out of the depths of the ocean up to the surface. The tunnel of mirror transformed as if it was dancing. Soon, a series of civilizations on different stars appeared one after another in picture scrolls. *Galaxy* changed back its form from a whale to its original one. Then, Agnes felt like she was on a super-high-speed maglev train that zipped forward.

The ship slowed down even more, and it felt like normal space travel. Before her eyes was a monitor showing a blue planet that looked slightly different from Planet Earth.

"Agnes, we are almost here. How did it feel to travel 2.3 million light-years?" the Lord asked Agnes.

"It only felt like 10–20 minutes have passed. Did I turn into an old, gray-haired grandma?"

"Not at all. You are still you."

The ship entered the atmosphere and slowly flew over an ocean. It landed on an abundantly green piece of land.

When Agnes got off the ship, animals and birds greeted her. They looked like the animals on Earth, but they spoke languages.

Captain Commander Z in his blackish outfit had turned into the figure of God Hermes.

A pathway paved with beautiful jewels appeared before their eyes. The pathway moved automatically, and they arrived at a Western-style building that looked like the White House.

"This was the house of Ame-no-Mioya-Gami

before he went to Japan 30,000 years ago," the Lord said.

"Well, it looks like an American building," Agnes said.

"There is a Japanese-style garden and a magnificent Japanese building like the Kinkakuji Temple behind it. The building in front of you is not the White House but a variation of the Lincoln Memorial."

On the left side of the Memorial stood a statue of Buddha that also looked like a *Kongo Rikishi* (Deva king) statue; on the right side stood a statue of U.S. President Lincoln.

They passed by the two statues and walked to the back. Agnes saw a view that certainly resembled the Kinkakuji Temple and its garden in Kyoto.

The pond in the garden looked very much like a pond in Kyoto with *nishikigoi* (brocaded carp) swimming in it, but what seemed to be the Kinkakuji Temple turned out to be more like a practical Japanese-style hotel. It was larger than the actual Kinkakuji Temple in Japan.

Agnes suddenly found herself dressed in a *furisode* (long-sleeved kimono for young women), and the Lord was dressed in a majestic kimono.

A beautiful woman wearing a lavender-colored dress came out of the house.

Before she knew it, Agnes found herself calling out to her—"Mother."

"My dear Panguru," the Lord said. "I have returned. I brought Agnes along. Or shall I call her, 'Suzu'?"

"Oh, Agnes is fine," Panguru said, as she turned to Agnes. "You have grown a lot. And we are about the same height. This is your home. Make yourself comfortable."

Large teardrops were flowing out of Agnes' eyes. Here, in the Andromeda Galaxy, another Earth existed 2.3 million light-years away.

9.

The Andromeda Galaxy is much larger than the Milky Way Galaxy containing Earth. Humans on Earth observe the Andromeda Galaxy and see that it is approaching the galaxy that contains their solar system; they speculate that the two galaxies will collide in three billion years and fully merge in five billion years.

The truth is that the Milky Way Galaxy is being pulled into the far larger Andromeda Galaxy.

M31 in the Andromeda Galaxy is not the name of a star. It is actually a mini-galaxy that exists within the Andromeda.

Planets of the solar system, including our Earth, are approaching M31 at a speed of 190 miles per second.

Now, the other Earth in the M31 Galaxy, where Agnes and the others landed, was known as "Mother." The name indicated that it was a mother planet that gave birth to various life forms. The planet was about 1.2 times the size of Earth, but its water, temperature, and atmosphere were no different from those on Earth. Gravity was almost identical. The small difference was that plants and organisms on Planet Mother grew at a somewhat faster rate. Many grains here were introduced to Earth and adapted there long ago. Likewise, many of the animals on this planet were like the prototypes of animals on Earth. And just like Earth, there was the North Pole, the South Pole, and the equator. Each continent had different climates, and some regions had four distinct seasons.

The current total population was about two billion, and the planet was split into three countries. Some people had migrated to past civilizations on Planet Earth from time to time, and many migrated to planets in other solar systems of other galaxies that had evolved to a sufficient level.

Planet Mother was also one of the five major planets that had been influencing Earth's civilization in our solar system.

Approximately 150 million years ago, Lord God descended onto Planet Earth under the name of "Elohim" to create a new Earth version of the El Cantare civilization and re-establish the standards of good and evil.

Since then, branch spirits of El Cantare and other ninth-dimensional spirits who had been acting as messiahs on various planets moved to Earth. These records were kept carefully on Planet Mother.

The Japanese pavilion in the shape of the Kinkakuji Temple, where Agnes and the others resided, stood on a slightly tall hill. She could look down and see an ocean nearby that seemed like Tokyo Bay. The capital was called Angel City, and it was home to about two million humanoid space people. Most of the administrative work and labor was done by robots. These robots had emotions similar to humans, and there were married couples and children. After gaining a certain level of experience, they were allowed to be born as humanoid space people on other planets. There were roughly three million robots.

El Cantare, Panguru, and Agnes were in a country called "Yamato."

The other two countries were called "Eagypt" and "Summerland." Eagypt was closely associated with the constellation Orion, and Summerland was closely associated with the constellation Lyra. Of course, Yamato, located on Planet Mother, had deep ties to Japan, Asia, and in ancient times, the Mu civilization on Earth.

When the spaceship *Andromeda Galaxy* landed in Japan approximately 30,000 years ago, they apparently landed as great giants, much bigger than their figures today. Their bodies were actually stretchable. The physiques they embodied were the same they used during a time period with many dinosaurs, so the ancient people of Japan immediately bowed down and worshiped them. However, it was apparently difficult for them to adapt to Earth's food, clothing, and shelter at first.

At her house, Mother Panguru showed Agnes a photo booklet that contained details from that time.

"I bet Father must have prepared for his descent, presuming that King Kong lived in Japan," Agnes said.

"There was no King Kong, but there seemed to have been mammoths and dragons that made their way from the continent. That's why they had to first demonstrate their strength," Panguru said.

"I wonder if the mammoths were bigger than elephants."

"I'd say so. Some people died trying to finish off a mammoth."

"By dragons, do you mean giant lizards?"

"They were descendants of dinosaurs from ancient times, but some of them could fly across the sky, whereas others were thick serpents with legs. Their numbers gradually declined through-out their battles against humans. They still live in the Spirit World, but now, whenever they are born on earth, they should be dwelling in human bodies."

"Mother, you had the ability to shapeshift, right?"

"I can turn into what looks like a panda's an-cestor, but it's not fit for moving around. So I can also turn into leopard form. It's a little sexy, you know? I can run at a speed of roughly 75 miles per hour, maybe like a cheetah."

"I heard that Father could transform into what looks like an enormous sumo wrestler, but does He have any other forms?"

"Your Father can transform into an enormous white elephant or a giant flying dragon covered in pure gold."

"You know, when I came to this planet using warp drive, I felt my body break down into molecules, atoms, photons, spiritons, and so on. I bet the third-dimensional physical body can transform into anything if the power of our mind becomes stronger, if our enlightenment level increases, and if our willpower reaches the power of creation. I need some practice."

"Oh, don't be stupid. You're capable of a Seraph transformation. Four wings will come out of you, and once you spin around, you will become like a whirlpool of flames. You're one of the four Seraphim who've been protecting Lord God with that. Don't you remember?"

"Oh, so that's the form I need to take so I can pass through the ninth-dimensional wall of flame and go to greet the Lord God."

Agnes wanted to learn many more things.

10.

The next day, Agnes decided to go on a tour of Planet Mother in a small "family UFO." The UFO was about 16 feet in diameter, and Agnes was accompanied by a male driver robot and a female guide robot.

The small UFO made an effortless departure from the garage in the backyard. There was an *RO* mark at the bottom of the UFO, which made it immediately known that anyone on board must be related to the planet's highest Master. The UFO probably had security guards in invisible mode.

Inside the bay area of Angel City was a gigantic monument—a *torii* gate modified in the shape of the alphabet "A." This seemed to be the place to make an interdimensional warp for a sortie.

To Agnes' surprise, the country of Yamato from the sky above took the shape of a large Shikoku Island with a cross on top of it. Or perhaps it looked like the continent of Australia with a cross-shaped wharf attached to it. Either way, it looked like the hidden bruise on her chest. It reminded her of the Shikoku-Island-shaped bruise on her pale white chest that had turned into a cross-shaped bruise after she received a mission from Jesus Christ. It was the symbol of Yamato— her home country on Mother, which was another Earth that sat in the solar system of M31 in the Andromeda Galaxy, 2.3 million light-years away.

Each pillar that stood below her eyes acted as a signpost for a ship arriving by sea or for a flying object departing to or arriving from another country.

From the sky, this country looked to be 70% green mountainous areas and 30% open plains, similar to Japan.

The blue sky had a large sun along with another sun which was yellow and somewhat smaller. The smaller sun revolved around the larger sun. The two suns brightened the planet, creating morning, noon, and evening.

The length of one day was about 29 hours, and the lengths of day and night varied with the season.

In general, plants probably grew faster than on Earth because of longer hours of sunlight. Semiannual and triannual planting, or double-cropping and triple-cropping, seemed to be the norm for rice and wheat. The country of Yamato on Planet Mother was abundant with water, and there were lakes, ponds, and rivers flowing in many locations.

The crucian carps in rivers and ponds grew to be roughly 3.3 feet long, and regular carps, or koi fish, grew to be roughly 10 feet long. A careless child would be swallowed up.

As she flew above the ocean, Agnes saw sperm whales and blue whales jumping above the surface as they spewed seawater. They looked like dolphins at first glance, but they were much larger than dolphins. Agnes saw a 50-foot-long giant squid wrapped around a roughly 65-foot-long whale and putting up a fight. *Prey of such size would make a good side dish for 80-foot-tall, sumo-wrestler-like humans during the age of Ame-no-Mioya-Gami.* Agnes chuckled at the thought.

She flew some more and saw Eagypt. It was a trapezoid-shaped continent. The coverage of green land was over about half of the area of the entire country of Eagypt, and there were large beasts along with animals such as deer, sheep, horses, and cows that were edible. Like in a safari park, all the animals were roaming around freely.

Eagypt had many pyramid-shaped altars that resembled the pyramids in various regions on Planet Earth. These pyramids ranged in height from several tens of feet to as high as 650 feet. Here, altar-type religions that were also prevalent on Earth continued to be practiced—or so it seemed.

Around the pyramids, there were radial streets like those in Paris. There was an arch that looked like the Arch of Triumph, so there must've been heroes like Napoleon in this country.

Not all great figures would act discreetly like my Father God, Agnes thought. She speculated that there were flamboyant aristocrats. Without being asked, the guide robot answered, "That's right."

Further south across the sea, a country called "Summerland" came into sight. Perhaps Russia would look like this under a temperate climate.

Looking down from the sky, there seemed to be a clear division between industrial and agricultural areas.

Some areas seemed to be military facilities. Agnes learned that since Planet Mother was sometimes invaded by outer space depending on the era, they conducted military drills. The guide robot explained that there were powerful fighters on Planet Zeta of the Magellanic Clouds and Beta Centauri, among others, and space wars took place several times. It further explained that as a result of these space wars, people fled to other planets and even retreated to Earth, where El Cantare had welcomed them as Earthlings many times. Thus, in the last few hundred million years, it seemed that El Cantare had set Planet Earth as a vital foothold.

Agnes returned home sometime in the evening.

Many people who had assisted Agnes in the past were gathered inside—a welcome party, perhaps.

Today, Mother Panguru was wearing a luxurious kimono, patterned with Mt. Fuji, a crane, and the sunrise on New Year's Day.

Relatives that seemed to be of various ethnic backgrounds were also gathered. The conversation topic mainly focused on the end of the

Seventh Civilization and the construction of the Eighth Civilization on Earth.

Some said, "Couldn't something have been done?" Others asked, "What will be the main teachings of the Eighth Civilization?"

An elderly person came out and said, "There's a way to go back in time and restart the last war. Take some light of archangels along with you from this country."

Father God spoke.

"I will have Agnes learn a little more about the universe. Then, it will restart."

11.

Several days had passed. Agnes heard that this planet also had hot springs, so she was looking forward to visiting one.

Around eight in the morning, however, she received a video call in her living room. Surprisingly, it was Mr. R. A. Goal.

Mr. R. A. Goal was the captain of the battleship *Enlightenment 1* during the war on Mars.

"Thank you for waiting," Agnes said to R. A. Goal.

"No problem. Sorry to call you without notice."

"You were a huge help back on Mars."

"You know, Lord El Cantare tells me He wants you to learn some more about the universe. Why don't you come to my place?"

"Oh! Is that alright with you?"

"You are very much welcome. But just to let

you know, the food tastes better where you are now. I don't want you to be disappointed."

"I don't mind the food."

"*Hehehe*. Then, I'll pick you up in my flying saucer around nine. Please be at the open space by your house."

As Agnes was getting ready with the help of Panguru, R. A. Goal's battleship—or rather, a large flying saucer about 650 feet in diameter—appeared about 100 yards away from them.

"Mother, isn't that too big?" Agnes asked.

"The destination is Planet Andalucia Beta in Ursa Minor, near the North Star. A large ship would be better suited for warp drive," Panguru said.

"By North Star, do you mean the star that's always up north when we look up the sky from Earth?"

"Don't tell me you've never heard of the Big Dipper. In China, it's said that Tiandi (the Emperor of Heaven) came from there. Your Father has been there before to guide the people there."

"Well, I'll be off for training," Agnes said, and she went out.

A staircase came out from the large flying saucer, and R. A. Goal personally made his way down to greet Agnes.

"Princess, please watch your step," R. A. Goal said.

"Please don't call me a princess. I'm only a clueless girl in her 20s."

The ship's interior was indeed smaller than that of *Andromeda Galaxy*, but it seemed comfortable near the control tower.

"Are you sure you're okay with using a battleship to pick me up?" Agnes asked R. A. Goal.

"This ship is the fastest, and it can engage in a battle if, by any chance, we encounter a dangerous force," R. A. Goal answered.

"Thank you very much for that. How long will it take to get to your planet?"

"It wouldn't be a normal operation. We are going to warp, so it might take around 15 minutes. Now, we'll be taking off."

Vrooom. With that, the ship floated up into the sky, passed through the A-shaped torii gate in the bay, and flew beyond the atmosphere.

The starry sky before her eyes began to flicker until they began to pass mirror glass after mirror glass of the torii gate. Everything inside the UFO became hazy and dissolved into thin air. Agnes felt that she, too, was becoming like golden sand and losing her human form.

Andalucia Beta in Ursa Minor, Andalucia Beta in Ursa Minor.

As Agnes repeatedly chanted this like a mantra in her mind, the ship sped up for roughly ten minutes and began to slow down for about five minutes. Once again, she saw something that looked like a path made of a mirror. Upon closer look, there were several stars on the outside of the ship and a galaxy at a distance.

The ship entered normal operation and headed into the planet's atmosphere. It would not burn up like a rocket capsule on Earth. This was because it was in a state of higher-dimensional existence until it could fly freely across the atmosphere.

Agnes soon realized that Andalucia Beta was a planet mainly with mountains. Unlike Planet Mother, this planet was 30% sea and 70% land, but the land areas were excessively mountainous.

As she looked down from the sky above, Agnes felt that living here would be somewhat difficult.

Shortly thereafter, a flat plain appeared in the middle of the mountains. There, the spaceship landed. It was a grassy plain. Agnes stepped out of the ship and saw a herd of animals that looked like goats and yaks. Apparently, these were animals that could live in mountainous areas of high altitudes. There were several water buffalos by a swamp nearby.

"The environment here is similar to that of the Himalayas, Nepal, and Tibet. The oxygen is a bit low, so you should chew this until you get used to it," said R. A. Goal, as he handed Agnes a piece of gum-looking thing.

The gum tasted cool and refreshing. Once she chewed it, oxygen seemed to generate inside her mouth.

R. A. Goal's space suit had changed into a dark red cloak enveloping his body. The cloak was like the color worn by monks climbing the Himalayas, and his hair was tied into a bun. His facial features started to look a lot like Shakyamuni Buddha.

The mountainside opened wide, and the battleship was stored there.

"You may be starting to understand. This planet is what we call a 'training planet,'" R. A. Goal explained. "The core members are those from various galaxies who have come here to become messiahs, along with ascetic monks to support them and robots to manage the animals on these mountains. The population is no more than that of a single village or a town. The living condition on this planet is so harsh that most people can't stand even two years. I am technically the Grand Master now, but El Cantare Himself used to teach here. This star is where we learn how to control our material desires and heighten our spiritual awareness. That's why we sometimes fast for about a week. We mainly eat sunflower seeds, grains of foxtail millets and barnyard millets, and beans, and sometimes we warm ourselves with goat milk and butter made out of that milk. Cheese made of goat milk can be our staple food, too. There's nothing here that's worth stealing, but we have a barrier in the sky that is hard to break in."

"Now, Agnes, let's see how many days you can endure before running off."

I've come to a tough place, Agnes thought to herself.

12.

Andalucia Beta in Ursa Minor. Agnes thought to herself, *I didn't know such a "training planet"— where one would train to become a messiah— existed in this romantic constellation containing the Big Dipper. Given that Father was once a Grand Master here, there must be a key here for me to grow from an archangel into a savior through living on this planet. What is it?*

They were in a room that was like a modified cave. In the middle was a furnace to warm themselves up or cook their meals. The floor was covered with straw that would serve as a carpet and sofa.

"Come here, R. A. One." Mr. R. A. Goal called out, and a boy who looked about 10 years old came out of the next door-less room. He had an adorable face. With his shaved head, he looked like a boy from a high-altitude village around Tibet. He seemed to be Mr. Goal's son.

"Well, I've been married before. But on a training planet like this, every woman runs off. There are mostly men here, and so this kid takes care of me," R. A. Goal said.

R. A. One quickly bowed to Agnes and began to prepare lunch.

"Today is your first day here, so we'll have a feast," R. A. Goal said to Agnes.

There was just one naked light bulb hanging from the ceiling, just like houses in Japan back in the first half of the 20th century. A hole was hollowed out in a rock, and there was a wooden door that covered it; at times, this door was raised up with a stick to let air and light in during the daytime.

The boy was cooking something in a small kitchen in the corner of the room. Soon, he carried over the dishes on a wooden plate. Agnes saw her lunch—a slice of cheese, a small sesame dumpling, and a bowl of yak butter tea. That was all. Lunchtime was over in three minutes.

On the other side of the kitchen, there was a "sink," or a half-round bamboo tube facing up like a gutter. The boy washed the bowls of their butter tea with running water that flowed through the rocks.

Agnes grunted. *Ugh. That was a feast?* All of a sudden, her thought flashed back to the ramen she ate in Sangenjaya, Tokyo.

The soy sauce ramen was ¥630 a bowl, I believe. The bamboo shoots were seasoned well and the boiled egg that was cut in half was delicious. After adding two or three sheets of seasoned seaweed, I would drink up the soup with a porcelain spoon and slurp up the noodles. There was steam from the soup too. Oh, I also can't forget the dumplings as a side dish!

Across the furnace, R. A. Goal was smirking as if he was trying to stifle a laugh.

"Ms. Agnes, you don't use money on this planet," R. A. Goal said.

"What? Then how do you go shopping?" Agnes asked.

"Everyone is self-sufficient."

I see how it is. Self-sufficiency. That means I have to make ramen noodles myself. Are there seasoned bamboo shoots here? How can I make the soup? As for seasoned seaweed, I'll have to collect seaweed from the ocean, dry it under the sun, and then process it. Hm, I'll need to find a chicken to get the egg. Dumplings are out of the question. There's no way I can make those.

All these things that crossed Agnes' mind momentarily were picked up by R. A. Goal.

"I'm sure life on Earth was convenient," R. A. Goal said. "But when you really think about it, life was also lavish there, wasn't it? That's why people are obsessed with convenience and consumption. There's no need to study and learn things by heart because you can look anything up on the smartphone. Money can buy anything. If you think you're simply paying ¥630 to the guy at the ramen shop, you're wrong. Many people make ingredients that go into the ramen, and there are distribution costs involved, too. Not one person lives their life thinking about these things. On this planet, you go back to the starting point and re-examine the greed within you. That's where your training starts."

Agnes was caught by surprise. *I thought I wasn't greedy, but in fact, I was full of greed. What people think of as advancement is actually deterioration. People today can't make anything on their own, yet they believe they are working just by operating computers. Most people can't even build those computers on their own. Argh, I have no words*. She let out a deep sigh.

"Yes, you are right," R. A. Goal continued. "Humans must start over by knowing the 'it's enough' mind. When life becomes too convenient, people no longer feel *gratitude*. Then, they forget to *give back* to others. They will no longer have appreciation for the favor they received from their parents, teachers, and other members of society or from their own country. Above all, they will lose respect for God and Buddha. Eventually, the desires that have swollen too much will give rise to excessive competition, leading the civilization to perish. Do you understand?"

Just then, R. A. One interrupted.

"Hey Sis, let's go collect ingredients for dinner."

Agnes felt slightly dizzy, but she followed the boy out of the house. Mountains were lined up in the far distance. The scenery was beautiful. The boy took Agnes' hand and ran up the mountain path. He carried a handbasket in his other hand.

"What should we have for dinner?" the boy asked Agnes.

"We have a choice?" Agnes asked.

"Depends on what we find, but I'll do my best for you, Sis."

A small field gradually came into their view. Purple corn grew there. The boy cheerfully hummed as he picked up six ears of corn.

Next, he tore off a cactus from between some rocks and put it in his basket. He also gathered a few flowers' worth of buckwheat nuts.

Finally, they went close to the water buffalos by the swamp. The boy took the bucket that was hanging from a nearby tree and milked a water buffalo, collecting the milk in the bucket.

"Sis, give it a try," he said. Agnes cautiously approached the water buffalo and tried milking it. It didn't go very well.

"Oh, I think this is the milk used to make mozzarella cheese. That one Italian restaurant was wonderful," Agnes muttered to herself.

When they got home, the boy crushed the corn kernels, rolled them into dumplings, and then stretched them out like pancakes between two iron plates. Both the cactus and buckwheat nuts were used as ingredients to add some flavor to the thin, baked cornbread. As expected, the water buffalo milk was poured into a pot and heated on a furnace as a substitute for soup.

13.

Night came. Agnes was told to sleep on a straw-covered wooden bed and wrap herself in a blanket made out of mountain goat fur. They gave off a slight smell of Mother Nature.

In the morning, Agnes drew water from a nearby well and wiped the room clean. She drank a warm glass of mountain goat milk for breakfast.

"Shall we start our training at eight o'clock?" Mr. R. A. Goal said.

They sat cross-legged on a cliff nearby with a splendid view to practice the "Meditation to Think Nothing."

Master Goal said, "Imagine yourself weighing zero grams. Visualize yourself flying through the air in your meditation posture, gliding to the lake over there and coming back."

The Master demonstrated just as he said. He floated about 20 inches off the ground, flew to the lake that was about 500 yards away, went around the lake, and returned.

Agnes didn't float a single inch off the ground. She thought, *Oh, it must be the enlightenment of "Matter is Void,"* but it was difficult for her to achieve zero gravity with her thoughts alone.

Next, Master Goal said, "Listen to the voice that cannot be heard."

That was also difficult. Agnes concentrated every nerve in her body on her hearing. She faintly sensed something like a thought from the chirping of a bird. But it never turned into words.

Master Goal then said, "A red carp in the lake will soon jump out of the water. Read its mind."

Indeed, 30 seconds later, a large red carp jumped out.

The carp's voice didn't reach Agnes.

"Looks like you're having a hard time. Alright then. There is a persimmon tree 30 feet away. Use your willpower to drop one of the persimmon fruits."

If it's willpower, I'm sure I can use some of it, Agnes thought. She concentrated all her will on a well-ripened persimmon. This time, the persimmon didn't fall, but a hole was made as if the fruit was shot by a pistol.

Agnes' stomach growled.

She had been hungry all morning.

"Alright now, I suppose that is it for today. Climb up the mountain and go find some sweet potatoes with my son."

R. A. One came over, and he swiftly ran up the mountain path. Agnes could barely keep up.

On the way up, a wild boar came out from a dwarf bamboo bush.

"Hey, can't we eat meat?" Agnes asked R. A. One.

"It's forbidden to kill."

"Then, I guess we'll have to look for sweet potatoes. Sweet potatoes will make for staple food."

But Agnes couldn't find any sweet potatoes. She dug up three yams with disappointment.

R. A. One came down the slope with about five sweet potatoes, roots and all.

They came back home, but Agnes didn't know how to eat the yams. She decided to wash them with water, peel off the skin, and cut them up like radish. It didn't seem like she could prepare the rice dish topped with grated yam.

R. A. One put the sweet potatoes on skewers and held them over the fire. After some time, Agnes smelled a sweet scent in the air. This was their lunch.

Master Goal spoke.

"Agnes, you don't need to feel impatient. The purpose of this training planet is to understand what it means to *live*. It's to awaken to the grace of God and to the preciousness of civilization and culture built upon by humankind in the past." "Once you awaken, it will open the way to gratitude and giving back. Then, it will lead to the next enlightenment: what it means to *let humankind live*." "Meditate over by that window. Picture your father and your mother in your mind, and thank them."

Agnes did as she was told.

She felt the gaze of merciful love from the Lord God.

She felt infinite love from her mother.

Perhaps it was an illusion, but Agnes felt as if hundreds of millions of years of history unfolded before her like a panorama. She felt that the "Past" was the "Present," and it was also the "Future."

That was all the training for the day.

On a different day, Master Goal began to teach the practice of bringing hail.

Just as Agnes saw the splash from a waterfall rise up in the sky, it turned into large drops of hailstones that fell one after another. It was the same work as that done by Father God. Agnes worked hard, and she was able to drop a few hailstones.

Next, Master Goal rained countless balls of fire from the blue sky.

All around, the shrubs on the mountainside began to catch fire.

Agnes, too, concentrated in her mind and tried unleashing fireballs from the sky.

The mountain burned even more.

Master R. A. Goal lifted the surface of the lake water about three feet into the air and brought it over the forest fire. The fire quickly went out.

"You seem to have a slightly higher talent for psychokinesis," R. A. Goal said to Agnes. "From now on, work on self-control, attain the enlightenment of egolessness, and train yourself to master the art of teleporting in an instant. You will eventually be able to warp between planets in the blink of an eye without the help of a spaceship."

On another day, training took place on a prairie.

"Today you will do combat training as a Seraph. Have a strong will to protect the Lord and try to show your true self."

After Agnes put her hands together in prayer, she began to spin. Then, four wings came out, and she was wrapped in flames. She ascended about 300 feet above the ground. When she emitted a laser beam onto the waterfall, the part below the water that was shot by the beam evaporated.

Next, Agnes emitted fireballs from her palms and fired at the rocky cliff. The surface of the cliff shattered, and the rocks tumbled down.

R. A. Goal acknowledged that Agnes made a certain level of improvement. All Agnes needed now was to hone her skills in an actual battle.

"Next, you'd better train yourself to fight malicious aliens under Commander Yaidron. If you encounter the Emperor of the dark-side universe, ask Father God for help," Master Goal said.

14.

R. A. Goal's son, R. A. One, was friendly and affectionate with Agnes, calling her "Sis." Agnes felt painful reluctance at the thought of saying farewell, but her first phase on the training planet was over. She was escorted back to Planet Mother in Andromeda.

Father God and Mother greeted her.

"You've lost weight," Mother Panguru said with a worried look on her face. "You must've lost at least 10 pounds."

That evening, Agnes was served a sea bream and a spiny lobster that were slightly larger than those on Earth. It had been a while since she last had such a feast.

"Food tastes really delicious after I disciplined myself on a training planet. I guess when we gorge ourselves on lots of food, we can't appreciate a good meal," Agnes said.

"That's also a learning experience," the Lord said. "When human beings become greedy, they are full of dissatisfaction and complaints. People who've forgotten the 'it's enough' mind will forget love and tolerance for other people."

Agnes told her parents that Master R. A. Goal advised her to start combat training with Mr. Yaidron, but Mother said, "Get some rest first."

Father God agreed and said, "Right now, Mr. Yaidron should be chasing down the emperor of the dark-side universe. With your strength now, Agnes, it's still too risky. Before you see him, head over to Mr. Metatron's place and learn more about 'Love.' No devil can defeat love. With spiritual power alone, you may win against the devil, but you could also lose."

Thus, the family of three decided to go to a hot spring resort on Planet Mother to get some rest for the time being.

The next day, they left their house on a medium-sized UFO. The country of Yamato on this planet also had hot springs.

After about a 5-minute flight, they saw a Konide-type mountain that looked like Mt. Fuji in Japan. It was apparently a volcano.

"That is called the 'Mountain of Immortality.' The word 'immortality,' *fuji* in Japanese, became the name of Mt. Fuji. It has great hot water. There is a special annex for our family behind the Ame-no-Mioya-Gami Shrine," the Lord said.

The three of them landed. After walking for a while, they came to a stone staircase with roughly 100 steps, and at the top of the stairs was the 'A'-shaped torii gate. When they passed through the gate, there were three roads approaching a shrine. The middle path was filled with marbles, to the left of it was a path paved with black cobblestones, and to the right of it was a path paved with white cobblestones. Agnes learned that the middle path was for gods to walk on, the left path was for human (space people) females to walk on, and the right path was for males to walk on.

The family walked along the marble path in the middle. After roughly 300 feet, Agnes saw a multistory architectural structure that looked like the Giant Wild Goose Pagoda among the trees. It was unclear what materials the structure was built of, but it appeared to be a seven-story structure, with clay-colored walls and a tiled roof on top of other clay-colored walls and a tiled roof, and so on.

Upon entering the building from the entrance on the first floor, Agnes saw a large statue, not of *Fudo Myoo*, or Acala, but more of *Nio* that looked like a sumo wrestler. The statue was 80 feet tall, and Agnes learned that it was modeled after Ame-no-Mioya-Gami, who landed on the foothills of Mt. Fuji 30,000 years ago.

"You were quite big back then, Father," Agnes said.

"Oh, how surprised the villagers were to see me so large with a 30-foot-long Japanese sword," the Lord said.

"Your Father showed them the majesty of God and taught them about faith tacitly with his presence," Panguru said.

"Mother, were you there?"

"At the time, you looked like a giant saber-toothed tiger and guarded me," the Lord said to Panguru. "Once the inhabitants calmed down, you changed form. You looked like the origin of *Princess Konohana-Sakuya*. I believe you called yourself 'Princess Prajna.'"

"Was that right?" Panguru said. "I didn't have the Wisdom of Prajna, so I might've been Princess Panda."

"Then the 'prajnaparamita' in the Heart Sutra would turn into 'panda-paramita,'" Agnes chimed in.

"Oh my, Agnes, stop making fun of your mother," Panguru said. "Shouldn't you be asking what your name was back then?"

"What? I wonder what it was. Maybe I was Princess Chimpanzee, ancestor of the Japanese macaque."

"I think it was Princess Suzuko," the Lord said. "You always wore a *suzu* (bell) on your hips since there were nasty bears every so often."

As the three of them chatted and laughed, they arrived at the annex.

They were greeted by a Japanese-looking proprietress and maids at the annex behind the shrine.

It was truly like a noble Japanese-style guest house.

They walked down a corridor and saw a fine Japanese garden outside a glass window.

Once they arrived at their room, there were

three open-air hot tubs, each partitioned with bamboo leaves.

One of the hot tubs was so large that it looked like a pond.

"The hot tub is more than 30 feet deep, and it's designed so that you can enjoy the hot spring in the form of Lord Ame-no-Mioya-Gami," the proprietress said. "Please go ahead and return to your natural form as the God enshrined in this temple to relax in the hot spring."

Agnes squealed in her heart. *Wow! I can't believe I came to the Mountain of Immortality and Gora Hot Spring of the Andromeda version.*

That night, Agnes ate a hearty meal and got plenty of rest on a fluffy futon mattress. They stayed for two nights and headed home.

Next up is Mr. Metatron's place, Agnes thought. *I wonder if he looks like Jesus Christ, given that he is part of Jesus Christ's soul and also his space soul. Or maybe he looks like a goat?*

What kind of place is Planet Include in the constellation Sagittarius? I was told that his wife, Madame Yamrozay, is like a sister to Mother Panguru. I also heard that her little sister, Semrozay, looks just like me and that she's an artistic soul who's talented at singing, dancing, and acting.

Agnes had learned that the constellation Sagittarius had the Southern Dipper, like the Big Dipper in Ursa Major. Long ago, in China, it was said that *sennins*, or hermits, of the Southern Dipper and the Big Dipper governed life and death, and they discussed with each other to determine the life span of a person. It was also believed that a wish for longevity was better made to the Southern Dipper. Agnes' next journey was about to begin.

Her heart pounded.

15.

There was no way for Agnes to easily find Planet Include of the constellation Sagittarius.

She had learned that to get to Sagittarius, it was a good idea to mark the Pistol Star that was observed toward the center of the Milky Way Galaxy where Earth belonged. The star was surrounded by a pistol-shaped nebula, and it was supposedly one of the heaviest stars, weighing 100 times more than the Sun.

Planet Include was not part of a large galaxy with beautiful spirals like the Milky Way, however. It was part of a dwarf galaxy that had an obscure shape. One could call this galaxy an irregular galaxy or a mini-galaxy. Even now, dwarf galaxies were on the verge of being engulfed by spiral galaxies.

Agnes had learned that Planet Include was situated in the dwarf irregular galaxy NGC 6822 within Sagittarius.

"Whatever happens, happens," Agnes told herself and decided to head to Planet Include with just a driver robot and a guide robot. This was also part of her training. She was told that in her small spaceship, it would take about three days to get there. Agnes had already worked so hard on the training planet, so she had to get used to solitude and space travel by now.

She began to accelerate her small-sized flying saucer that was designed for space travel. Then, the cosmos began to flicker. It was as if the stars were dancing.

"So the direction of the Pistol Star that's toward the center of the Milky Way and weighs 100 times more than the Sun is…" As Agnes muttered under her breath, the Pistol Star's coordinates appeared on the panel.

"Let's just try. Small flying saucer, warp now!"

Agnes' spaceship was about to collide with a large planet, but the flying saucer had become squishy by expanding and contracting as if it was being reflected in a bumpy mirror. So it went straight through the planet. It couldn't really be called a warp.

Agnes raised her voice and shouted, "Triple-speed warp!"

The flying saucer was powered by Agnes' psychokinesis—it had no fuel or engine. It was as if she was flying a paper airplane in the Great Universe at zero gravity. She had no choice but to set her mind on a destination and concentrate her mind: "Just fly." She already possessed psychokinesis that was strong enough to fly a small-sized flying saucer to reach Earth. In the worst-case scenario, she would have to send out an SOS signal to Mr. Metatron or Father God.

Agnes kept calling Mr. Metatron's name in her mind. Metatron, as seen with her mind's eye, sometimes looked like a mountain goat, whereas at times, he looked like Jesus Christ. Agnes assured herself that he wouldn't abandon a woman with the cross, as Metatron was one of Jesus' space souls to begin with.

A green planet came into sight as Agnes was getting exhausted.

"*That* is Planet Include," the guide robot said. "Good oxygen levels. 60% ocean and 40% land. Most of the land is grassland, and there are forests in mountainous areas. Planet Include is about 80% the size of Earth. Many herbivores live here, and there also seem to be more than 500 million humanoid space people."

Eventually, they flew over a region resembling European forests and saw a town on a prairie containing many brick houses.

Agnes started to see a 10-foot-tall goat-faced figure standing in the town's central square wearing a red cape and brown boots.

The flying saucer landed, and Agnes walked down the ramp. Mr. Metatron had large obsidian eyes and two horns that stretched backward. His mouth was somewhat goat-like, but his hands were like those of a human.

Behind him stood two women. On the far back was perhaps his wife Yamrozay. She slightly resembled Mother Panguru. The other young woman was most likely Semrozay. She looked like Agnes but with longer hair.

"So the women are humanoid?"

Agnes blurted out an insensitive question from the start.

"Welcome, Agnes. I was out until a while ago. I'll change into a humanoid when I get home," Metatron said.

"I wish I could meet Mrs. Panguru, too. We used to work together often," Yamrozay said.

"I'm working on a new song right now. Why don't you join me later?" Semrozay said.

The four of them—Panguru, Agnes, Yamrozay, and Semrozay—looked similar. *Perhaps we are the four Seraphim*, Agnes thought. *I wonder if Father cut corners and made us look alike.*

They walked for about three minutes until they reached a Western-style brick building. Four or five helper robots were moving around.

"What's your impression of Planet Include?" Metatron asked Agnes.

"It feels like Germany, although I've never been there."

"Actually, it should look like Rome in Italy, but I guess the forests, prairies, and brick houses give off a feeling of Germany," Metatron explained. "There are no megacities like Tokyo, in Japan, on Planet Include. Where we are now is the only city with over a million people, and the rest are cities having 500,000–700,000 people. Ms. Agnes, you must be tired. And you must be hungry."

The spacious living room was made of logs, and it contained a burgundy sofa, a wooden table with chairs, and a fireplace. A candle chandelier hung in the center of the ceiling. Agnes had a feeling that a philosopher would fancy such a house.

"There's a big church nearby, and my husband gives a sermon every Sunday," Yamrozay said.

"What kind of sermon?" Agnes asked.

"He teaches a lot about love and tolerance. Maybe it resembles Christianity on Earth."

"I also sing or play piano there sometimes. There's also a real choir, which I'm not a part of," Semrozay said.

The helper robots brought stew and a long, thin loaf of bread with a crispy crust along with café au lait for each person there. Soon, it was lunch.

An exploration of Planet Include was about to begin.

Agnes was hardly able to contain her excitement.

16.

There was a relatively large church near Metatron's mansion. Its normal capacity was around 1,000 people, but taking the second floor into account, nearly 2,000 believers could be accommodated. The church was similar to the churches in Europe from the Middle Ages, but the difference was that it could simultaneously broadcast videos to satellite relay halls around the planet. Key lectures given by messiahs on other planets were often relayed as well. That was the reason why large UFO fleets would always appear in the sky whenever El Cantare gave a grand public lecture on Earth. His lectures were relayed from the UFOs above the venue to their respective mother planets.

Despite this indisputable fact of the universe, the Japanese government had officially announced that there was not a single UFO report. If the pilots of the Japan Air Self-Defense Force and those of airlines such as JAL and ANA reported UFO sightings, they were transferred to ground duty; so everyone remained silent. Even if a fleet of UFOs was caught on radar, the Self-Defense Forces never scrambled because they'd find nothing by the time they reached the sky.

Such backward ignorance about UFO information was probably one of the reasons the Lord God deemed the civilization on Earth unsuitable for the space age.

If people did not acknowledge the existence of human souls or UFOs, it would mean that they were lagging behind the 30,000-years-ago Japan. Allowing eight billion people to be born under such materialistic scientism would only lead to the explosive expansion of hell's population. There were things that couldn't be saved, even with the power of Agnes and the others. From the perspective of the universe, restarting was more meaningful than making amendments.

On a Sunday immediately following Agnes' arrival, Metatron's lecture was titled "The Reason for Earth's Destruction." It was awfully persuasive. The United States of America had announced 143 possible UFO sightings, and a public hearing was held for the first time in 50 years, but only one sighting was examined. The only conclusion was that it was an unknown, fast-flying object.

The then U.S. administration must've been convinced that it was a new weapon of Russia, China, or North Korea because these countries had already developed hypersonic missiles. It was a big deal for the United States to fall behind them in missile technology, and it stirred fear among the Americans. The United States "successfully" tested a hypersonic missile for the third time, a year-and-a-half ahead of its schedule, but it only succeeded in reaching Mach 5 and above.

Generally, Mach 5 and above, or more than five times the speed of sound, was called hypersonic. But if Russia, China, and North Korea had missiles of Mach 8, Mach 10, or Mach 20, it would be impossible for the United States to intercept them. An ordinary missile ranged from Mach 2 to Mach 3, so it could shoot down fighter jets, bombers, and commercial airliners, but an ordinary missile couldn't hit an ICBM unless it was aimed at the peak of the projectile after the ICBM left the atmosphere.

Even against low-flying, zigzag missiles, which China and North Korea were thought to have, and any ballistic missile that flew at the speed of Mach 8 or Mach 10 and above, PAC-3 and Aegis Ashore were completely useless.

It was only natural for the U.S. Air Force to suspect Russia, China, and North Korea were sharing alien technology.

The UFO images on radar were moving at hypersonic speeds, so they were a threat indeed—whether they were of Earthlings or aliens.

Generally speaking, UFOs of the Space Federation were able to shoot down even a Mach 20 missile, but they couldn't make attacks unless Earthlings established their own standard of justice. In general, El Cantare's permission was required in advance, but Earthlings' faith in God was as thin as paper; they were only interested in worldly life and pleasure. They had no idea what God was thinking, so voting rates and audience ratings were worshiped in the place of "God's justice" in mass media democracy.

At times, God's justice includes protecting the poor and the weak.

But God's Will lies in valuing equality of opportunity over equality of outcome; it does not accord with His Will to punish those who make self-help efforts as evil people and exploit them. "Fairness" is another criterion of judgment for God.

And as long as humankind doesn't believe in God and Buddha and in heaven and hell, and doesn't understand the essence of altruism, it is difficult for them to accurately judge the righteousness of a war.

In addition, mere sympathy is not the same as love. "Sympathy" is needed on the premise that this world is the "school for souls," but viewing the corruption of the soul—caused by one's own impiety, immorality, and crime—in light of the law of cause and effect, is a different story.

Metatron gave such fundamental teachings using Earth as an example.

At the same time, Metatron ran a school for underprivileged children and a hospital near his church. He also trained many priests who served God. Thus, Metatron had multifaceted feelings.

17.

Even after returning to his mansion, Metatron continued to teach Agnes about the importance of love—the love of those with an evil heart will always be accompanied by the desire to benefit themselves and have hypocrisy hidden in it. That is why people need to check and see if they are not craving praise from others; if they do not have a desire for fame; if they have not forgotten the heart to seek justice and the heart to draw a line between public life and private life. The authenticity of one's "love" is always put to the test.

Yamrozay chimed in.

"Personally speaking, the teaching of 'forgiving love' is the most appealing to me. The hard part is to not let evil escalate."

Semrozay followed after Yamrozay.

"For me, I think of love as entertaining others and making them happy. But it's hard to know how much spirit of self-sacrifice I really have. It's wonderful to be friends with everyone and live harmoniously, but will I be able to forgive other people's sins? Would I be able to hold on to my faith even if I were to be nailed to the cross or must give up my life? I do have doubts that come with my young age. How about you, Ms. Agnes?"

Agnes felt that everyone on this planet was like a philosopher.

"I suffered from a sexual crime on Planet Earth, but I awakened to faith and I was saved. I was given supernatural powers, too, but I couldn't even save my own life. I died once. Thanks to the Lord God's words, however, I was granted another life on earth. Then, I realized that the 'prosperity' of those who have lost faith, who are drowned in materialism and are manipulated by the devils, was the road to hell. In the end, I couldn't pass judgment on good and evil to save Earth's Seventh Civilization. I felt I was lacking in my abilities. That's why I'm now starting over and learning from the messiahs of the universe."

"Struggling between love and justice is a difficult challenge no leader can avoid," Metatron said to Agnes. "You are about to take on a great battle once more. It's the battle against evil gods of the dark-side universe. This must be a test for you to become a certified messiah, given that Father God gave you this assignment. My wish is for you to learn from this planet that the power of love conquers evil."

As he spoke, Mr. Metatron seemed like a godly Jesus Christ—but blonde.

"I have a cross-shaped stigma on my chest. Does this mean that I should learn from Jesus Christ's martyrdom?"

"I think you've learned the art of a Seraph from Master R. A. Goal. The very way you live your life will guide the future generations. The 'cross' of the space age will not be the same cross of Jesus Christ at the Jewish Golgotha. However, you must leave behind your life as an epic for posterity, for the people of the universe. Once again, you will experience a great battle that may cost you your life. At that time, protect your life with the heart of love that I taught, just like a turtle's shell. Show them that there is still a Light of Hope in this universe. About 70% to 80% of this universe is made of dark matter, but you must show that Light is stronger than darkness. You must condemn and correct the arrogance of the evil gods of the dark-side universe."

Agnes clearly understood that the essence of her training on this planet was to learn the teachings of the mind. After all, knowledge is power.

Because experience was important in everything, she asked Semrozay, who was around her age, to give her a detailed tour around Planet Include.

Planet Include was not as rich as her home planet, Mother, but it was not as harsh of an environment as R. A. Goal's training planet. Here, it seemed that the main training was to study the Truth, in a decently affluent environment, and help people get back on their feet through the power of words. Agnes learned that people worked some kind of job for five days a week and partook in volunteering or music festivals on Saturdays and Sundays.

Semrozay seemed to spend her weekdays studying literature and music while creating new poems or songs and sending them to various people throughout space. Sometimes, she would take trips to other planets with Master Metatron for research. At times, she would even fight against malicious aliens who plotted to invade Earth. Agnes learned from Semrozay how to fly a small-sized UFO and how to fight against the enemy.

Semrozay looked a lot like Agnes as if they

were twins. But Semrozay seemed to have greater physical abilities. When they went to the training fields in unpopulated mountainous areas, Agnes learned from Semrozay how to flip around the UFO, how to improve the accuracy of the laser beam gun, and how to use missiles. Agnes learned that she should know the ways to escape from the enemy—such as instant teleportation of the UFO while in it and how to instantaneously get to a safe place on her own if her flying saucer was destroyed. She also learned how to use the art of "mind-reflecting" against opponents that tried to control her mind, how to see through the lure of the Pleiadians' witchcraft that used their beauty and sexual charms, and how to become thoughtless to protect her faith from Vegans' art of shapeshifting and magic.

Furthermore, Agnes heard that Semrozay trained both her mind and body from time to time with activities like kickboxing. Agnes was advised to learn some kind of combat skill that was useful for an individual battle. She decided to ask Father to teach her the art of the sword.

Agnes, with newly added strength, returned to the Lord and Panguru.

Father God asked her, "What did you learn?" She answered, "I learned the importance of studying and training. I need to study Buddha's Truth to give teachings to people, and it's important to have a lifestyle that will always serve as a role model for other people. I also understood that physical training is a key to heightening my mental energy."

Agnes then said, "Father, please teach me the art of the sword."

Father modified a building near their house into a dojo.

Agnes started by swinging a wooden sword, then a bamboo sword. Father said that a bad posture was proof that swinging practice was not enough; if she couldn't stand straight, she couldn't sit straight. He said that those were the issues she had to overcome even before practicing the art of the sword. Sometimes, Mother Panguru trained her by acting as her opponent during attack-defense training. A month later, Agnes began training with a real sword, which was a lightsaber like those used in *Star Wars* movies.

Agnes sensed that the time was drawing closer.

18.

Finally, it was time to ask Mr. Yaidron, another certified messiah, for a lesson. Mr. Yaidron seemed to be originally based in the Magellanic Clouds. The Magellanic Clouds weren't visible from Japan, but once you traveled to countries in the southern hemisphere such as Australia and New Zealand, you could see two galaxies—one large and one small—in the sky near the south celestial pole. The Large Magellanic Cloud was an irregular galaxy located 160,000 light-years away from Earth. There was an immense Tarantula Nebula nearby. The other galaxy was the Small Magellanic Cloud that was 200,000 light-years away.

Both galaxies were relatively close to Earth, given that M31 in the Andromeda Galaxy, to which Father God's mother planet belonged, was 2.3 million light-years away.

Of the twin planets in the Small Magellanic Cloud—Planet Zeta and Planet Elder—Mr. Yaidron was from Planet Elder. Planet Zeta and Planet Elder had a long history of space war with each other. Originally a Reptilian combat species, the people of Zeta were overwhelmingly aggressive in space; they showed up in various galaxies to destroy the people of numerous planets. There was a turn of events, however, when a savior named Yaidron was born on its twin planet, Planet Elder. Since then, the people of Zeta began losing ground and escaped to other planets that were inhabited by herbivorous space people. Some of the Zeta people even came to Earth in an attempt to invade, but after being defeated by Mr. Yaidron and the Lord God, some of them converted to faith-minded Reptilians and became Earthlings.

However, Mr. Yaidron was currently at the Martian base. He had captured one of the enemy

commanders, Ahriman, and the plan was to interrogate Ahriman while using him as a decoy to
lure their commander-in-chief, Kandahar, and his
mastermind leader. It was a rather bold strategy
because he was purposefully inviting an attack on
the Martian base.

Thus, Agnes decided to first return to the
Martian base and go see Commander Yaidron.
Flagship *Andromeda Galaxy* would be mobilized
from Planet Mother of Andromeda only when
it was time for the main battle, so instead, the
semi-main battleship, Space Battleship *Mikasa*,
was mobilized for her. *Mikasa* was about 820 feet
long. It was not shaped like a flying saucer, but it
looked like a lean version of Earth's Battleship
Yamato—fitting for the country of Yamato. The
head of the ship was Commander Z. They were
prepared for any real battle that could take place.

Agnes arrived at the Martian base on Battleship *Mikasa*, headed by Captain Commander Z, along with a fleet of roughly 50 other ships.

Based on Mr. Yaidron's investigative report, the enemy general, Kandahar, should sense the slightest SOS signal emitted by Ahriman; it was highly likely that Kandahar would launch an attack on the Martian base within a few days.

But Mr. Yaidron's real aim encompassed a grander strategy. He had to find out if there was someone pulling the strings behind the forces of the dark-side universe and where their base and its entrance were.

There is a term known as "multiverse." To put it more simply, it is about a "parallel universe." The idea is that there exists a "flip-side universe" that is separate from the universe where human beings are living on several planets including Earth. Another version of ourselves supposedly live in this flip-side universe, and although they follow different evolutional paths, there are several "holes" that allow us to go back and forth between the two worlds. If that is true, attacking enemy bases in the main universe is not enough because the real enemy power is preserved in the flip-side universe.

Recently, there have been more supporters for this idea of the multiverse. The newest *Doctor Strange* movie is set on the premise that there are many versions of Dr. Strange in multiple universes. It can be regarded as a nightmare, or rather, a drug addiction, but it is a possibility. There has already been the idea that a person's soul siblings reside in the Spirit World and the idea that your other self resides in another galaxy. Perhaps it will be possible to assume that some kind of flip-side-universal-existence created the realm of hell within the Spirit Worlds of Earth and other planets. If this is the case, the standards of good and evil can become inverted, and heaven and hell can even be reversed.

Perhaps the end of the Seventh Civilization on Earth described in *The Unknown Stigma 2 <The Resurrection>* had to happen because more than half the spirits of Earthlings were heading to hell, and unless saviors or archangels worked hard to prevent them from going there and led them to be purified, part of the front-side universe could eventually be taken over and ruled by the flip-side universe. Given that the humanoid space people on other planets were fewer in numbers, Earth, with over eight billion people, was a considerably large, important ground for soul training.

On that note, maybe it was necessary to destroy Earth's human race for now; they had forgotten their faith in the God of the front-side universe and were multiplying in numbers while carrying values that were against God.

Now, the multiverse theory was somewhat difficult for Agnes to comprehend, but she could relate to the idea that a flip-side universe existed as part of their parallel universe.

That was why Agnes was determined to unite people of the front-side universe with faith in the Lord God and devotion to His teachings. Those from the flip-side universe would have to be sealed to the other side of the "holes," and if not, their plots to invade the front-side universe had to be utterly destroyed.

At any cost, I must prevent people from worshiping what we think of as the devil as the new God.

I want to make this universe into the kind of place where people with many different senses of values can co-exist under the belief in the One and Only God.

Right now, those were the thoughts that Agnes concentrated on.

All of a sudden, she received a report that the enemy army appeared and was heading over to the base on Mars.

It must've been part of their plan to rescue Ahriman, their general who had fought many battles on their behalf. This meant that there would be an invasion on the Martian base, in addition to the battle in outer space. Commander Z and Agnes had to prepare for infiltrators into the base, leaving General Yaidron to fight enemies outside of the base. Ahriman's isolation tower was located at the tip of the Manhattan-like city. Thus began a special guard formation. Would the barriers of their base be breached? Would Agnes' training prove effective? A battle was about to begin.

19.

A large enemy fleet appeared above Mars. There were probably 500 ships. This time, the defending Yaidron fleet had about 300 ships, so they were outnumbered; however, Commander Yaidron's true intention was to make the enemy think that they had the upper hand, thereby making them overconfident and conceited. Thus, Yaidron had factored in and prepared for some damage.

In the battle between the two sides' small-sized UFOs operated by Greys, there was a 50-50 damage dealt to both sides.

The enemy's main force was the battleship *Death Strong* that was most likely led by Kandahar. Yaidron's flying saucer, *God Fire*, was about 660 feet in diameter. Agnes shuddered as she locked her eyes on the monitor and saw *Death Strong*—also a battleship, but much, much larger—to be over 1,600 feet in diameter. She anxiously wondered whether they could win without Father's *Andromeda Galaxy*.

Commander Z, who stood to her right, said, "This base itself has anti-aircraft cannons and missiles and other secret weapons, too. Just when the enemies think they've won, we'll turn the tables."

But intensive attacks with their three cruisers were not enough to break through the barriers of the enemy battleship, *Death Strong*.

In addition to *Death Strong*, there were two other ships that protected each side of the flagship: a 1,000-foot-class missile battleship, *My Turn*, and a battleship called *Thunder Bolt* with electric shock artilleries. From the allied forces, 50 of the 100-foot-class destroyers fired missiles all at once. However, these missiles were caught one after another by the casting-net-like electric shock beams of the battleship *Thunder Bolt*. The missiles fell inert.

Next, *My Turn* fired missiles, and ally destroyers scattered in all directions; once the destroyers were locked on and tracked, however, over half of them were shot down.

"There's nothing we can do," Agnes said.

Just then, two cannons came out from the front of Yaidron's *God Fire* and fired an aqua-blue laser beam.

The aqua-blue laser beam headed straight for *Thunder Bolt*.

Surprisingly, once the laser beam struck *Thunder Bolt*, the metal on the surface of the flying saucer began to freeze. "Oh, they won't be able to use their electric shock artilleries now," Agnes whispered.

She was spot-on. Yaidron's ship launched two rings of light that looked like wheels and hit the now-frozen *Thunder Bolt*. Their battleship broke into three pieces and fell, making small explosions along the surface of Mars.

The enemy was angered, and they fired two nuclear missiles from their battleship toward Yaidron's spaceship. Yaidron's ship flipped around and began to soar at a rapid speed. The two nuclear missiles chased his ship. At an altitude of 16,000 feet, Yaidron's ship came to a stop, turned off all power, and began to free-fall. The enemy battleship, *My Turn*, was caught by surprise. After all, they were directly underneath Yaidron's *God Fire*. The homing missiles chased the heat source of the enemy aircraft, so the fact that Yaidron's spaceship turned off its power and began to free-fall meant that the nuclear missiles would pass by his ship and hit *My Turn* instead.

Commander Yaidron muttered, "It's my turn." The captain of the enemy ship was caught off-guard, so he made a taboo move: escaping sideways at full speed. Unfortunately, the missile flew at a faster speed than the enemy battleship.

As a last resort, *My Turn* tried to warp away. But it would take at least one minute to set up a warp. Two of their brandish high-performance nuclear missiles hit their ship. It was as if giant fireworks exploded in the sky above Mars. The second enemy battleship was destroyed.

All that remained was a one-on-one battleship duel between the enemy flagship, *Death Strong*, and Yaidron's spacecraft.

"Mr. Yaidron is a skilled fighter," said Agnes, as she sighed in relief.

Just then, the sound of sirens echoed throughout the base.

"Enemy in, enemy in," an announcement rang.

"So they are here," Commander Z muttered. "It must be part of their plan to rescue Ahriman. The combat above Mars must be a diversionary tactic."

"What's a diversionary tactic?" Agnes asked.

"It's to attack the main target while drawing the enemy's attention somewhere else."

The two of them boarded Space Battleship *Mikasa*.

It seemed that about five mole-shaped tanks broke through the ceiling above the Martian base, which was located underground. Of course, their target was Ahriman's detention tower at the tip of Manhattan.

Roughly 30 small-sized UFOs were mobilized to intercept the mole-shaped tanks, which had foldable wings and drills attached to the front. While the UFOs dealt with the tanks, ninja-like aliens parachuted down onto the rooftops and streets all around.

Now, how should they fight? Space Battleship *Mikasa* awaited in the sky above the tip of Manhattan.

Most of the mole-shaped tanks were shot down by the beams of small UFOs, but the ninja-like aliens had already shapeshifted into Martians. It was impossible to launch an attack on them from the battleship.

Agnes, Commander Z, and about a dozen fighters made a soft landing near Ahriman's detention tower. From now onward, they had to engage in hand-to-hand combat using laser beam guns and lightsabers. The fruit of Agnes' training sessions would be put to the test.

Agnes was dressed in a combat uniform, carrying a laser beam gun on her right hip, and a lightsaber on her left.

The enemy force's laser beam guns were fired from an opposite building. A shoulder-fired bazooka was fired from the left side of the building, destroying a part of the walls of the detention tower.

Can I win in my first hand-to-hand combat engagement? Agnes remembered the days of her training with Master R. A. Goal and R. A. One.

Oh, I would give anything to get through this and see R. A. One again.

That was Agnes' honest feeling.

20.

Agnes fought the three space ninjas with a light-saber. Her first strike was a quick slash, and she certainly felt that she landed a hard hit. Against the second ninja, she slashed diagonally down from his right shoulder. The training at the home dojo proved to be effective.

The third ninja jumped down from the balcony on the second floor. Agnes quickly turned around and gave a counterstrike to his body, followed by a diagonal slash from behind his back.

Meanwhile, Commander Z was facing a large man wearing a gray outfit. He fired a laser beam gun, but the ray was deflected. Black poison needles were shot from the opponent's 10 fingers on his hands. Commander Z's outfit was partially torn off. The opponent was tough to beat. Commander Z quickly stripped off his black outfit and transformed into a glowing form of God Hermes.

He soared above the sky with his large white wings, and the Hermes sandals on his ankles accelerated his ascent. On his left hand was the almighty staff of Kerykeion, emitting gold light.

His opponent, however, had also transformed. He had taken off his 10-foot-long gray outfit and turned into a great pterosaur that was at least 50 feet long. It was most likely a Reptilian from Altair, the counterpart of Vega located in the constellation Lyra. He was probably one of the chiefs of the species that resisted becoming faith-minded Reptilians.

The two of them engaged in aerial combat for a while. Eventually, Hermes' staff of Kerykeion emitted a lightning bolt that overpowered his opponent, and the pterosaur's wings were torn apart. Still, the pterosaur continued to blow flames as large as 25 feet from its mouth.

"Don't you know that I'm actually God?" said God Hermes, as he emitted a thick laser beam from the palm of his right hand. The pterosaur turned ash black, and he collapsed in a veil of smoke.

Agnes was also facing her next tough opponent, however. At first, she thought her opponent was a female fighter, but she transformed into a giant octopus. It was over 30 feet tall with eight tentacles.

The voice of Metatron's wife, Yamrozay, echoed in Agnes' heart:

"Agnes, your opponent is an anti-Seraphim soldier. Be careful. But that octopus-type was designed to defeat me, and I believe you have a new weapon."

Agnes' laser beam gun wasn't effective. And no matter how many times she chopped off the octopus' tentacles with her lightsaber, new ones kept regenerating.

"Screw it, I'm going to make enough *takoyaki* (octopus dumplings) for 10,000 Martian soldiers," said Agnes, as she became empowered to defeat her opponent once again. But Agnes was pulled in by the octopus' suckers and restrained by the tentacle, and she dropped her lightsaber.

I remember Mr. Metatron telling me to be like a turtle and protect myself with a heart of love. If I hide inside the shell of a sea turtle, I can't be defeated no matter how tightly the octopus binds me.

Agnes wished in her mind to transform into a sea turtle. She pulled her head, arms, and legs inside. The turtle began to spin and chop off the octopus' tentacles. Soon a four-winged Seraph appeared and created a whirlwind of flames. The giant cephalopod became a grilled octopus and fell to the ground.

Only a few more enemies remained. The Martian soldiers were ahead in the fight.

Then, it happened. With a sudden roar, one of the artificial suns was blown away. The enemy battleship, *Death Strong*, had broken through the ceiling and appeared over the city of Mars.

Just before that, the enemy ship had dived down to launch a *kamikaze* attack on Yaidron's *God Fire*. Yaidron's spaceship quickly changed into a perpendicularly rotating flying saucer and vertically split in half to dodge *Death Strong*'s onslaught. The enemy ship, however, without batting an eye at Yaidron's ship, fired its main laser beam cannons and missiles as it broke through the transparent dome covering the surface of Mars. It used the momentum to charge into the underground city. Many people fled the scene when the tremendously large hull of *Death Strong* broke through the defensive lines and made its imposing appearance above the New York-type city of Mars. The battleship headed for the tip of Manhattan, raising two strands of black smoke.

Space Battleship *Mikasa* was on standby, however, which caught the enemy by surprise.

Under Vice Captain Kuropatkin's order, the three main cannons of *Mikasa* blew fire. Three drill-type rotating shells hit the enemy ship. The shells rotated as they burrowed through *Death Strong* and exploded inside. As the enemy warship tilted at an angle of 45 degrees, it began to catch fire. Just like that, the enemy warship slammed into the twin towers—the World Trade Centers—destroying El Cantare's memorial buildings. Small explosions erupted continuously inside the enemy battleship, even under the rubble.

To the allies' surprise, however, the enemy commander-in-chief, Kandahar, had already teleported into Ahriman's detention tower in Battery Park. Kandahar was a tyrannosaurus-type alien with two heads. Imagine Godzilla with two heads—that was Kandahar. Powerful laser beams were fired from the eyes, two on each of the two heads, knocking out the guards. Kandahar made a hole in the building, and he stormed into Ahriman's room.

It was around that time when a medium-sized flying saucer, about 160 feet in diameter, separated from *Death Strong*, which was thought to be in flames, and came out into the air from under the fallen twin towers.

Kandahar rescued Ahriman and teleported onboard the medium-sized ship, *Death Match*. The control center of the flagship had been another UFO. It must've been designed in advance so that they could escape with *Death Match* in case their larger ship was destroyed. *Death Match* rapidly ascended and flew out the opening in the ceiling of the underground city.

God Hermes transformed back into Commander Z and boarded *Mikasa*. Agnes joined him. They chased down *Death Match*.

In the sky immediately above, Yaidron's *God*

Fire was on standby. Yaidron fired four missiles from the rear of his ship. Commander Z, who was chasing the enemy ship, also fired four missiles from below. *Death Match* was hanging by a thread—or so it should've been.

The eight missiles fired from both sides collided with each other and exploded, while the flying saucer that carried Kandahar and Ahriman disappeared into thin air.

"They warped away, as I thought." Yaidron chuckled. He was calm.

21.

Yaidron kept his eye on the entire solar system with a space radar. A considerable amount of damage was inflicted on the enemy side, so he thought that the warp destination for a 160-foot, medium-sized ship would be nearby.

"There it is." Yaidron let out in a whisper. A bright dot had appeared near Saturn. "It must be *Death Match*," he told himself and contacted *Mikasa*. They decided to make a short-distance warp from Mars to the sky above Saturn. Saturn had 64 satellites, both big and small. Most of them were small, icy satellites, but Titan was by far the largest that shined eighth magnitude, and then there was the mysterious sponge-like satellite Hyperion that was oval in shape and 220 miles in long diameter. The surface of Titan was similar to Mars, so the passageway to the dark-side universe could be Hyperion.

The two spaceships, *God Fire* and *Mikasa*, warped into the vicinity of Saturn. The enemy had yet to realize that they were being followed. They switched over to invisible camouflage mode and approached Saturn's satellite Hyperion.

This peculiar sponge-like satellite had a number of large holes in it. The enemy dived into one of them.

"That's it. That's the tunnel into the parallel universe." Yaidron, Commander Z, and Agnes headed into a hole, about 1.2 miles in diameter, of the spooky satellite Hyperion.

It was obviously dark inside the hole, but it was swirling like the Naruto whirlpool of Shikoku Island, Japan. *God Fire* and *Mikasa* pushed forward for more than five minutes amidst the eerie grinding and creaking of the ships' bodies.

Then, the two ships emerged from the hole. For a moment, they saw *Death Match* floating in space.

But that wasn't the end. All three ships were sucked in one direction by a powerful magnetic force. Commander Z shouted, "It's a black hole!" It is said that when the sun dies, it becomes a black hole, and no light can escape due to its huge mass. They had never heard of anyone coming back alive after being sucked into a black hole. Yaidron found out that they were being sucked into a black hole in the center of the Sombrero Galaxy, M104, in the constellation Virgo. Everyone lost consciousness for a few minutes. Once they regained their awareness, their ships were once again floating in outer space.

Yaidron recognized the familiar view. They were in the Small Magellanic Cloud. There were twin planets in front of him: Planet Elder and Planet Zeta. Had he returned to his home? But something was wrong. From the reddish planet, Zeta, a large fleet was about to invade Planet Elder. *Death Match* escaped into the fleet.

He got a message from Commander Z, saying, "Is this Elder your planet?" It was certainly the same planet, but the greens were darker.

The large fleet of ships from Planet Zeta was nuking Planet Elder. Cities throughout Elder were burning.

"This is World War III from 30 years ago. This war brought Elder on the verge of becoming colonized. But, then, I appeared..." Yaidron was speechless. *Kandahar and Ahriman came from Planet Zeta in the past, flew through the black hole, and appeared 30 years later in the solar system*, he thought.

Soon, General Yaidron should emerge from Planet Elder for his first battle and wipe out the enemy. Yaidron realized that the two enemy generals who he had destroyed 30 years ago had time-warped and attacked Earth and Mars. It was only 30 years ago on Planet Elder; nonetheless, on Earth, it could've been several thousands of years ago or perhaps even before that. Time was uncertain when they passed through a black hole that would absorb even light with its colossal mass. The history of the universe wasn't linear.

Shortly thereafter, General Yaidron from the past made an appearance in his battleship, *God's Not Dead*, and inflicted considerable damage to the Zeta assailants who were mostly Reptilians.

"I get it now," Commander Z said. "These Zeta space people appeared on ancient Earth, were struck down by the Creator God Alpha, and joined faith-minded Reptilians on Earth, huh. Kandahar and Ahriman went to Earth after invading other planets."

"Can't we alter the history of the universe?" Agnes asked. "If we had killed them here, maybe Earth would've been safe."

No one but El Cantare could answer this question. Once you destroyed the source of the devils, the historical record of Earth up to the Seventh Civilization would also be rewritten.

Suddenly, Father God's *Andromeda Galaxy* appeared out of the blue.

"All of you, that is enough for this mission. I now dare say to you. I am the one who put good and evil against each other to compete in the universe, thereby setting the stage for humankind to abandon evil, choose good, and gain wisdom. Yes, indeed, the clash between good and evil will not end as long as the universe evolves. But I'll say unto you: I have raised many saviors and archangels along the way. We shall return home."

With His words, *Andromeda Galaxy*, accompanied by *God Fire* and *Mikasa*, time-warped 30 years forward to Planet Mother in the Andromeda Galaxy.

Panguru was delighted to hear that everyone was coming back after a long time away. She had even invited R. A. Goal and R. A. One to their house in the country of Yamato on Planet Mother.

"Strawberry mochi is yummy. I want to try making it too," R. A. One said.

Yaidron looked flustered that he let the enemy go.

Metatron comforted him by saying, "Sometimes love is to forgive your enemy. They provide learning experiences, after all."

Yamrozay, who looked like the Japanese actress Yuriko Yoshitaka, comforted Commander Z and Agnes. She said, "It's important to be proud of yourself for putting up a good fight."

Semrozay asked, "Agnes, you're leaving once again to create the Eighth Civilization on Earth, right?"

"That's the plan, but I don't think I'm fit to be a goddess," Agnes replied. She then got up from her seat and said, "Oh! I need to write a letter to my friend on Earth." She went to another room to write a letter, gave the letter to a pigeon-type robot, and sent it toward Earth.

End of the story.

22.

R. A. One came to visit Panguru again.

"Where's Sis?" He asked Panguru. She responded, "Agnes is going to create a new civilization on a place called Earth in the solar system."

"What's for dinner?"

"Have you heard of it? It's called *nikujaga*. You stew potatoes, carrots, onions, small pieces of artificial meat, and shirataki noodles in soy sauce and sugar."

"I'm not allowed to kill, so I don't think I can have beef," R. A. One said with a look of disappointment.

"I already told you, that's why we're having artificial meat today. Artificial meat is made from soybeans. I didn't use beef or pork."

"Why did you make *nikujaga*?" asked the little boy.

"Well, this country called Japan on Planet Earth once fought against the Russian Baltic Fleet. A great man named Heihachiro Togo achieved a 'perfect game.' That's how Japan won against Russia."

"What's a perfect game?"

"It means that the Baltic Fleet, renowned as the world's strongest fleet, was utterly defeated by Commander-in-Chief Heihachiro Togo of Japan using the 'Crossing the T' tactic."

"Wow, Mr. Togo must be strong like Mr. Yaidron."

"That's right. Mr. Togo beat Russia when they were 10 times more powerful than Japan."

"Was he strong because he ate *nikujaga*?"

"When he was younger, Mr. Togo studied in England for five years. It's said that when he returned to Japan, he came up with a dish called *nikujaga*. That's why I wanted to cook it for you."

"I think I'll make some *nikujaga* for Agnes one day."

"Uh-huh. Before you do that, we have to deliver seed potatoes to the new Planet Earth. Agnes went to the New Mu Continent. Maybe it doesn't have any potatoes yet."

"I'll be sure to deliver them," R. A. One said with great enthusiasm.

Here, on the New Mu Continent of Planet Earth, plants and trees had finally started to grow. Fishing was relatively feasible, but farming required time and energy to construct the fields and rice paddies.

Nevertheless, the people who had drifted here from all over the world were motivated to start a new civilization, bringing a variety of things with them.

Naoyuki Yamane, former chief of the Metropolitan Police Department's First Criminal Investigation Division, and Haruka Kazami, former chief of the Public Security Bureau, were digging up the soil to build a modest truncated pyramid. The pyramid was 30 feet long on each side and about 50 feet tall. It became Grecian when they added stone stairs.

"Based on Agnes' letter, she should be descending here soon to this New Mu Continent on Earth," Yamane said.

"Yep, it's been almost one month," Kazami responded.

"You know, she would look quite powerful as a god if she became a thousand-year-old grandma," Yamane said.

"Oh, stop it. Based on the calculation of my University-of-Tokyo-brain, Agnes hasn't aged at all."

"What kind of formula did you use?"

"Well, it's my '*hunch*-puter'."

The two of them had anticipated that Agnes would descend from heaven as a god, so they quit their jobs as police officers and decided to become the country's first priests. Soon came the twilight of the seventh day of July.

An enormous UFO appeared in the sky, rotated as it radiated golden light, and came to a complete halt above the truncated pyramid that Yamane and Kazami had built.

The central base of the flying saucer opened, and a divine figure slowly descended.

About 300 people gathered around to watch. Yamane played the role of a priest and Kazami played the role of a shrine maiden, as they awaited the new god to descend from the sky.

"Here is the descent of Goddess Agnes!" cried Yamane.

Agnes wore a red cloak and a silver tiara. She was covered in white, lacy clothing. Then, she slowly descended to the divine throne.

Kazami cried, "Here is Goddess Agnes!"

Several Japanese whispered, "Isn't she the Sun Goddess Amaterasu-O-Mikami?"

On Agnes' chest, however, a diamond cross was shining brightly.

"O Jesus!" the English speakers exclaimed.

"Whatever's fine with me," Agnes said. Yamane and Kazami bowed down with a chuckle.

It was the descent of the goddess. Even if Jesus came as a woman, no one would complain.

Agnes trembled with excitement.

Thus, the night of July 7 became the anniversary of the god's descent on earth.

Agnes voiced the first words toward the people: "Love your Lord God El Cantare." Her words contained deep conviction.

THE END

ABOUT THE AUTHOR

Founder and CEO of Happy Science Group.

Ryuho Okawa was born on July 7th 1956, in Tokushima, Japan. After graduating from the University of Tokyo with a law degree, he joined a Tokyo-based trading house. While working at its New York headquarters, he studied international finance at the Graduate Center of the City University of New York. In 1981, he attained Great Enlightenment and became aware that he is El Cantare with a mission to bring salvation to all humankind.

In 1986, he established Happy Science. It now has members in over 165 countries across the world, with more than 700 branches and temples as well as 10,000 missionary houses around the world.

He has given over 3,450 lectures (of which more than 150 are in English) and published over 3,000 books (of which more than 600 are Spiritual Interview Series), and many are translated into 40 languages. Along with *The Laws of the Sun* and *The Laws Of Messiah*, many of the books have become best sellers or million sellers. To date, Happy Science has produced 25 movies. The original story and original concept were given by the Executive Producer Ryuho Okawa. He has also composed music and written lyrics of over 450 pieces.

Moreover, he is the Founder of Happy Science University and Happy Science Academy (Junior and Senior High School), Founder and President of the Happiness Realization Party, Founder and Honorary Headmaster of Happy Science Institute of Government and Management, Founder of IRH Press Co., Ltd., and the Chairperson of NEW STAR PRODUCTION Co., Ltd. and ARI Production Co., Ltd.

WHAT IS EL CANTARE?

El Cantare means "the Light of the Earth," and is the Supreme God of the Earth who has been guiding humankind since the beginning of Genesis. He is whom Jesus called Father and Muhammad called Allah, and is *Ame-no-Mioya-Gami*, Japanese Father God. Different parts of El Cantare's core consciousness have descended to Earth in the past, once as Alpha and another as Elohim. His branch spirits, such as Shakyamuni Buddha and Hermes, have descended to Earth many times and helped to flourish many civilizations. To unite various religions and to integrate various fields of study in order to build a new civilization on Earth, a part of the core consciousness has descended to Earth as Master Ryuho Okawa.

Alpha is a part of the core consciousness of El Cantare who descended to Earth around 330 million years ago. Alpha preached Earth's Truths to harmonize and unify Earth-born humans and space people who came from other planets.

Elohim is a part of El Cantare's core consciousness who descended to Earth around 150 million years ago. He gave wisdom, mainly on the differences of light and darkness, good and evil.

Ame-no-Mioya-Gami (Japanese Father God) is the Creator God and the Father God who appears in the ancient literature, *Hotsuma Tsutae*. It is believed that He descended on the foothills of Mt. Fuji about 30,000 years ago and built the Fuji dynasty, which is the root of the Japanese civilization. With justice as the central pillar, Ame-no-Mioya-Gami's teachings spread to ancient civilizations of other countries in the world.

Shakyamuni Buddha was born as a prince into the Shakya Clan in India around 2,600 years ago. When he was 29 years old, he renounced the world and sought enlightenment. He later attained Great Enlightenment and founded Buddhism.

Hermes is one of the 12 Olympian gods in Greek mythology, but the spiritual Truth is that he taught the teachings of love and progress around 4,300 years ago that became the origin of the current Western civilization. He is a hero that truly existed.

Ophealis was born in Greece around 6,500 years ago and was the leader who took an expedition to as far as Egypt. He is the God of miracles, prosperity, and arts, and is known as Osiris in the Egyptian mythology.

Rient Arl Croud was born as a king of the ancient Incan Empire around 7,000 years ago and taught about the mysteries of the mind. In the heavenly world, he is responsible for the interactions that take place between various planets.

Thoth was an almighty leader who built the golden age of the Atlantic civilization around 12,000 years ago. In the Egyptian mythology, he is known as god Thoth.

Ra Mu was a leader who built the golden age of the civilization of Mu around 17,000 years ago. As a religious leader and a politician, he ruled by uniting religion and politics.

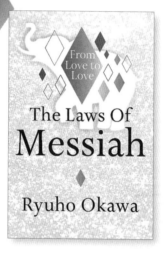

The
28th
Laws
Series

The Laws Of Messiah
From Love to Love

Paperback • 248 pages • $16.95
ISBN: 978-1-942125-90-7 (Jan. 31, 2022)

"What is Messiah?" This book carries an important message of love and guidance to people living now from the Modern-Day Messiah or the Modern-Day Savior. It also reveals the secret of Shambhala, the spiritual center of Earth, as well as the truth that this spiritual center is currently in danger of perishing and what we can do to protect this sacred place.

Love your Lord God. Know that those who don't know love don't know God. Discover the true love of God and the ideal practice of faith. This book teaches the most important element we must not lose sight of as we go through our soul training on this planet Earth.

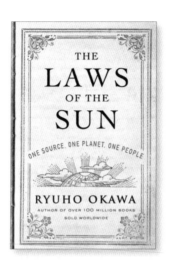

THE LAWS OF THE SUN

ONE SOURCE, ONE PLANET, ONE PEOPLE

Paperback • 288 pages • $15.95
ISBN: 978-1-942125-43-3 (Oct. 15, 2018)

Imagine if you could ask God why he created this world and what spiritual laws he used to shape us—and everything around us. In *The Laws of the Sun*, Ryuho Okawa outlines these laws of the universe and provides a road map for living one's life with greater purpose and meaning. This powerful book shows the way to realize true happiness—a happiness that continues from this world through the other.

DISCOVER THE TRUTH BEHIND THE MYSTERY

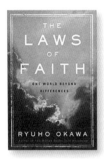

THE LAWS OF FAITH

ONE WORLD BEYOND DIFFERENCES

Paperback • 208 pages • $15.95
ISBN: 978-1-942125-34-1 (Mar. 31, 2018)

Ryuho Okawa preaches at the core of a new universal religion from various angles while integrating logical and spiritual viewpoints in mind with current world situations. This book offers us the key to accept diversities beyond differences to create a world filled with peace and prosperity.

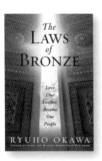

THE LAWS OF BRONZE

LOVE ONE ANOTHER, BECOME ONE PEOPLE

Paperback • 224 pages • $15.95
ISBN: 978-1-942125-50-1 (Mar. 15, 2019)

This is the 25th volume of the Laws Series by Ryuho Okawa. This miraculous and inspiring book will show the keys to living a spiritual life of truth regardless of their age, gender, or race.

R. A. GOAL'S WORDS FOR THE FUTURE

MESSAGES FROM A SPACE BEING
TO THE PEOPLE OF EARTH

Paperback • $11.95 • ISBN: 978-1-943928-10-1
E-book • $10.99 • ISBN: 978-1-943928-11-8

R. A. Goal, a certified messiah from Planet Andalucia Beta in Ursa Minor, gives humans on Earth three predictions for 2021. They include the prospect of the novel coronavirus pandemic, the outlook of economic crisis, and the risk of war. But the hope is that Savior is now born on Earth to overcome any bad predictions. Now is the time to open our hearts and listen to the words from R. A. Goal.

THE DESCENT OF JAPANESE FATHER GOD AME-NO-MIOYA-GAMI

THE "GOD OF CREATION" IN THE ANCIENT
DOCUMENT *HOTSUMA TSUTAE*

Paperback • $14.95 • ISBN: 978-1-943928-29-3
E-book • $13.99 • ISBN: 978-1-943928-31-6

By reading this book, you can find the origin of bushido (samurai spirit) and understand how the ancient Japanese civilization influenced other countries. Now that the world is in confusion, Japan is expected to awaken to its true origin and courageously rise to bring justice to the world.

SPIRITUAL MESSAGES FROM METATRON LIGHT IN THE TIMES OF CRISIS

Paperback • 146 pages • $11.95
ISBN: 978-1-943928-19-4 (Nov. 4, 2021)

Metatron is one of the highest-ranked angels (Seraphim) in Judaism and Christianity, and also one of the saviors of universe who has guided the civilizations of many planets including Earth, under the guidance of Lord God. Such savior has sent a message upon seeing the crisis of Earth. You will also learn about the truth behind the coronavirus pandemic, the unimaginable extent of China's desire, the danger of appeasement policy toward China, and the secret of Metatron.

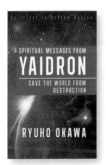

SPIRITUAL MESSAGES FROM YAIDRON SAVE THE WORLD FROM DESTRUCTION

Paperback • $11.95 • ISBN: 978-1-943928-23-1
E-book • $10.99 • ISBN: 978-1-943928-25-5

In this book, Yaidron explains what was going on behind the military coup in Myanmar and Taliban's control over Afghanistan. He also warns of the imminent danger approaching Taiwan. What is now going on is a battle between democratic values and the communist one-party control. How to overcome this battle and create peace on Earth depends on the faith and righteous actions of each one of us.

The Unknown Stigma Series

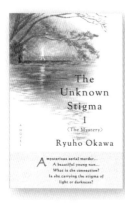

Published on October 1, 2022

The Unknown Stigma 1
<The Mystery>

Hardcover • 192 pages • $17.95
ISBN: 978-1-942125-28-0

The first spiritual mystery novel by Ryuho Okawa. It happened one early summer afternoon, in a densely wooded park in Tokyo: following a loud scream of a young woman, the alleged victim was found lying with his eyes rolled back and foaming at the mouth. But there was no sign of forced trauma, nor even a drop of blood. Then, similar murder cases continued one after another without any clues. Later, this mysterious serial murder case leads back to a young Catholic nun...

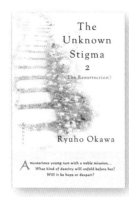

Published on November 1, 2022

The Unknown Stigma 2
<The Resurrection>

Hardcover • 180 pages • $17.95
ISBN: 978-1-942125-31-0

A sequel to *The Unknown Stigma 1 <The Mystery>* by Ryuho Okawa. After an extraordinary spiritual experience, a young, mysterious Catholic nun is now endowed with a new, noble mission. What kind of destiny will she face? Will it be hope or despair that awaits her? The story develops into a turn of events that no one could ever have anticipated. Are you ready to embrace its shocking ending?

NEW TITLES

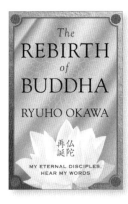

Published on August 15, 2022

THE REBIRTH OF BUDDHA

MY ETERNAL DISCIPLES,
HEAR MY WORDS

Paperback • 280 pages • $17.95
ISBN: 978-1-942125-95-2

These are the messages of Buddha who has returned to this modern age as promised to His eternal beloved disciples. They are in simple words and poetic style, yet contain profound messages. Once you start reading these passages, your soul will be replenished as the plant absorbs the water, and you will remember why you chose this era to be born into with Buddha. Listen to the voices of your Eternal Master and awaken to your calling.

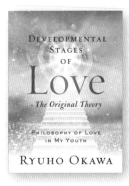

Published on June 15, 2022

DEVELOPMENTAL STAGES OF LOVE - THE ORIGINAL THEORY

PHILOSOPHY OF LOVE IN MY YOUTH

Hardcover • 200 pages • $17.95
ISBN: 978-1-942125-94-5

This book is about author Ryuho Okawa's original philosophy of love which serves as the foundation of love in the chapter three of *The Laws of the Sun*. It consists of series of short essays authored during his age of 25 through 28 while he was working as a young promising business elite at an international trading company after attaining the Great Enlightenment in 1981. The developmental stages of love unites love and enlightenment, West and East, and bridges Christianity and Buddhism.

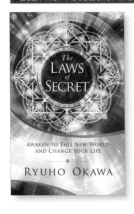

THE LAWS OF SECRET

AWAKEN TO THIS NEW WORLD AND CHANGE YOUR LIFE

Paperback • 248 pages • $16.95
ISBN: 978-1-942125-81-5 (Apr. 20, 2021)

Our physical world coexists with the multi-dimensional spirit world and we are constantly interacting with some kind of spiritual energy, whether positive or negative, without consciously realizing it. This book reveals how our lives are affected by invisible influences, including the spiritual reasons behind influenza, the novel coronavirus infection, and other illnesses. The new view of the world in this book will inspire you to change your life in a better direction, and to become someone who can give hope and courage to others in this age of confusion.

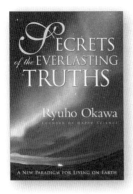

SECRETS OF THE EVERLASTING TRUTHS

A NEW PARADIGM FOR LIVING ON EARTH

Paperback • 144 pages • $14.95
ISBN: 978-1-937673-10-9 (Jun. 16, 2012)

Okawa offers a glimpse of the vast universe created by God and discloses that humanity is intimately guided by celestial influences. Our planet will experience a decisive paradigm shift of "knowledge" and "truth," culminating in an era of paradoxical spirituality, where mastery of science will depend on spiritual knowledge. The advancement that we seek, resides within us.

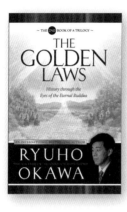

THE GOLDEN LAWS

HISTORY THROUGH THE EYES OF THE ETERNAL BUDDHA

E-book • 201 pages • $13.99
ISBN: 978-1-941779-82-8 (Jul. 1, 2011)

Throughout history, Great Guiding Spirits have been present on Earth in both the East and the West at crucial points in human history to further our spiritual development. *The Golden Laws* reveals how Divine Plan has been unfolding on Earth, and outlines 5,000 years of the secret history of humankind. Once we understand the true course of history, through past, present and into the future, we cannot help but become aware of the significance of our spiritual mission in the present age.

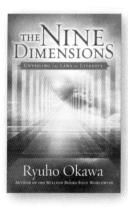

THE NINE DIMENSIONS

UNVEILING THE LAWS OF ETERNITY

Paperback • 168 pages • $15.95
ISBN: 978-0-982698-56-3 (Feb. 16, 2012)

This book is a window into the mind of our loving God, who designed this world and the vast, wondrous world of our afterlife as a school with many levels through which our souls learn and grow. When the religions and cultures of the world discover the truth of their common spiritual origin, they will be inspired to accept their differences, come together under faith in God, and build an era of harmony and peaceful progress on Earth.

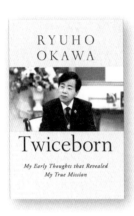

TWICEBORN

MY EARLY THOUGHTS THAT REVEALED MY TRUE MISSION

Hardcover • 206 pages • $19.95
ISBN: 978-1-942125-74-7 (Oct. 7, 2020)

This semi-autobiography of Ryuho Okawa reveals the origins of his thoughts and how he made up his mind to establish Happy Science to spread the Truth to the world. It also contains the very first grand lecture where he declared himself as El Cantare. The timeless wisdom in Twiceborn will surely inspire you and help you fulfill your mission in this lifetime.

THE NEW RESURRECTION

MY MIRACULOUS STORY OF OVERCOMING ILLNESS AND DEATH

Hardcover • 224 pages • $19.95
ISBN: 978-1-942125-64-8 (Feb. 26, 2020)

The New Resurrection is an autobiographical account of an astonishing miracle experienced by author Ryuho Okawa in 2004. This event was adapted into the feature-length film *Immortal Hero*. Today, Okawa lives each day with the readiness to die for the Truth and has dedicated his life to selflessly guiding faith seekers towards spiritual development and happiness.

OTHER RECOMMENDED TITLES

THE DESCENT OF ELOHIM
Spiritual Messages for the Movie,
The Laws of the Universe - The Age of Elohim

MY JOURNEY THROUGH THE SPIRIT WORLD
A True Account of My Experiences of the Hereafter

THE LAWS OF JUSTICE
How We Can Solve World Conflicts and Bring Peace

THE POSSESSION
Know the Ghost Condition and
Overcome Negative Spiritual Influence

THE REAL EXORCIST
Attain Wisdom to Conquer Evil

PUTIN'S REAL INTENTIONS
ON UKRAINE INVASION
Interview with the President's Guardian Spirit

TRUMP SHALL NEVER DIE
His Determination to Come Back

INSIDE THE MIND OF PRESIDENT BIDEN
Thoughts Revealed by His Guardian Spirit
Days before His Inauguration

For a complete list of books, visit <u>okawabooks.com</u>

MUSIC BY RYUHO OKAWA

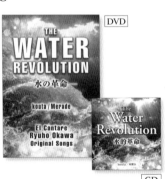

With Savior *English version*

This is the message of hope to the modern people who are living in the midst of the Coronavirus pandemic, natural disasters, economic depression, and other various crises.

Search on YouTube

[**with savior** 🔍] for a short ad!

The Thunder

a composition for repelling the Coronavirus

We have been granted this music from our Lord. It will repel away the novel Coronavirus originated in China. Experience this magnificent powerful music.

Search on YouTube

[**the thunder composition** 🔍]

for a short ad!

The Exorcism

prayer music for repelling Lost Spirits

Feel the divine vibrations of this Japanese and Western exorcising symphony to banish all evil possessions you suffer from and to purify your space!

Search on YouTube

[**the exorcism repelling** 🔍]

for a short ad!

Listen now today!

 Download from
Spotify **iTunes** **Amazon**

DVD, CD available at amazon.com, and Happy Science locations worldwide

ABOUT HAPPY SCIENCE

Happy Science is a global movement that empowers individuals to find purpose and spiritual happiness and to share that happiness with their families, societies, and the world. With more than 12 million members around the world, Happy Science aims to increase awareness of spiritual truths and expand our capacity for love, compassion, and joy so that together we can create the kind of world we all wish to live in.

Activities at Happy Science are based on the Principle of Happiness (Love, Wisdom, Self-Reflection, and Progress). This principle embraces worldwide philosophies and beliefs, transcending boundaries of culture and religions.

Love teaches us to give ourselves freely without expecting anything in return; it encompasses giving, nurturing, and forgiving.

Wisdom leads us to the insights of spiritual truths, and opens us to the true meaning of life and the will of God (the universe, the highest power, Buddha).

Self-Reflection brings a mindful, nonjudgmental lens to our thoughts and actions to help us find our truest selves—the essence of our souls—and deepen our connection to the highest power. It helps us attain a clean and peaceful mind and leads us to the right life path.

Progress emphasizes the positive, dynamic aspects of our spiritual growth—actions we can take to manifest and spread happiness around the world. It's a path that not only expands our soul growth, but also furthers the collective potential of the world we live in.

PROGRAMS AND EVENTS

The doors of Happy Science are open to all. We offer a variety of programs and events, including self-exploration and self-growth programs, spiritual seminars, meditation and contemplation sessions, study groups, and book events.

Our programs are designed to:

* Deepen your understanding of your purpose and meaning in life
* Improve your relationships and increase your capacity to love unconditionally
* Attain peace of mind, decrease anxiety and stress, and feel positive
* Gain deeper insights and a broader perspective on the world
* Learn how to overcome life's challenges
  ... and much more.

For more information, visit <u>happy-science.org</u>.

CONTACT INFORMATION

Happy Science is a worldwide organization with branches and temples around the globe. For a comprehensive list, visit the worldwide directory at *happy-science.org*. The following are some of the many Happy Science locations:

UNITED STATES AND CANADA

New York
79 Franklin St., New York, NY 10013, USA
Phone: 1-212-343-7972
Fax: 1-212-343-7973
Email: ny@happy-science.org
Website: happyscience-usa.org

New Jersey
66 Hudson St., #2R, Hoboken, NJ 07030, USA
Phone: 1-201-313-0127
Email: nj@happy-science.org
Website: happyscience-usa.org

Chicago
2300 Barrington Rd., Suite #400,
Hoffman Estates, IL 60169, USA
Phone: 1-630-937-3077
Email: chicago@happy-science.org
Website: happyscience-usa.org

Florida
5208 8th St., Zephyrhills, FL 33542, USA
Phone: 1-813-715-0000
Fax: 1-813-715-0010
Email: florida@happy-science.org
Website: happyscience-usa.org

Atlanta
1874 Piedmont Ave., NE Suite 360-C
Atlanta, GA 30324, USA
Phone: 1-404-892-7770
Email: atlanta@happy-science.org
Website: happyscience-usa.org

San Francisco
525 Clinton St.
Redwood City, CA 94062, USA
Phone & Fax: 1-650-363-2777
Email: sf@happy-science.org
Website: happyscience-usa.org

Los Angeles
1590 E. Del Mar Blvd., Pasadena, CA 91106, USA
Phone: 1-626-395-7775
Fax: 1-626-395-7776
Email: la@happy-science.org
Website: happyscience-usa.org

Orange County
16541 Gothard St. Suite 104
Huntington Beach, CA 92647
Phone: 1-714-659-1501
Email: oc@happy-science.org
Website: happyscience-usa.org

San Diego
7841 Balboa Ave. Suite #202
San Diego, CA 92111, USA
Phone: 1-626-395-7775
Fax: 1-626-395-7776
E-mail: sandiego@happy-science.org
Website: happyscience-usa.org

Hawaii
Phone: 1-808-591-9772
Fax: 1-808-591-9776
Email: hi@happy-science.org
Website: happyscience-usa.org

Kauai
3343 Kanakolu Street, Suite 5
Lihue, HI 96766, USA
Phone: 1-808-822-7007
Fax: 1-808-822-6007
Email: kauai-hi@happy-science.org
Website: happyscience-usa.org

Toronto

845 The Queensway
Etobicoke, ON M8Z 1N6, Canada
Phone: 1-416-901-3747
Email: toronto@happy-science.org
Website: happy-science.ca

Vancouver

#201-2607 East 49th Avenue,
Vancouver, BC, V5S 1J9, Canada
Phone: 1-604-437-7735
Fax: 1-604-437-7764
Email: vancouver@happy-science.org
Website: happy-science.ca

INTERNATIONAL

Tokyo

1-6-7 Togoshi, Shinagawa,
Tokyo, 142-0041, Japan
Phone: 81-3-6384-5770
Fax: 81-3-6384-5776
Email: tokyo@happy-science.org
Website: happy-science.org

Seoul

74, Sadang-ro 27-gil,
Dongjak-gu, Seoul, Korea
Phone: 82-2-3478-8777
Fax: 82-2-3478-9777
Email: korea@happy-science.org
Website: happyscience-korea.org

London

3 Margaret St.
London, W1W 8RE United Kingdom
Phone: 44-20-7323-9255
Fax: 44-20-7323-9344
Email: eu@happy-science.org
Website: www.happyscience-uk.org

Taipei

No. 89, Lane 155, Dunhua N. Road,
Songshan District, Taipei City 105, Taiwan
Phone: 886-2-2719-9377
Fax: 886-2-2719-5570
Email: taiwan@happy-science.org
Website: happyscience-tw.org

Sydney

516 Pacific Highway, Lane Cove North,
2066 NSW, Australia
Phone: 61-2-9411-2877
Fax: 61-2-9411-2822
Email: sydney@happy-science.org

Kuala Lumpur

No 22A, Block 2, Jalil Link Jalan Jalil
Jaya 2, Bukit Jalil 57000,
Kuala Lumpur, Malaysia
Phone: 60-3-8998-7877
Fax: 60-3-8998-7977
Email: malaysia@happy-science.org
Website: happyscience.org.my

Sao Paulo

Rua. Domingos de Morais 1154,
Vila Mariana, Sao Paulo SP
CEP 04010-100, Brazil
Phone: 55-11-5088-3800
Email: sp@happy-science.org
Website: happyscience.com.br

Kathmandu

Kathmandu Metropolitan City,
Ward No. 15, Ring Road, Kimdol,
Sitapaila Kathmandu, Nepal
Phone: 977-1-427-2931
Email: nepal@happy-science.org

Jundiai

Rua Congo, 447, Jd. Bonfiglioli
Jundiai-CEP, 13207-340, Brazil
Phone: 55-11-4587-5952
Email: jundiai@happy-science.org

Kampala

Plot 877 Rubaga Road, Kampala
P.O. Box 34130 Kampala, UGANDA
Phone: 256-79-4682-121
Email: uganda@happy-science.org

ABOUT IRH PRESS

HS Press is an imprint of IRH Press Co., Ltd. IRH Press Co., Ltd., based in Tokyo, was founded in 1987 as a publishing division of Happy Science. IRH Press publishes religious and spiritual books, journals, magazines and also operates broadcast and film production enterprises. For more information, visit *okawabooks.com*.

Follow us on:

f Facebook: Okawa Books   ⊙ Instagram: OkawaBooks

▶ Youtube: Okawa Books   🐦 Twitter: Okawa Books

𝓟 Pinterest: Okawa Books   g Goodreads: Ryuho Okawa

——— **NEWSLETTER** ———

To receive book related news, promotions and events, please subscribe to our newsletter below.

⊘ eepurl.com/bsMeJj

——— **AUDIO / VISUAL MEDIA** ———

YOUTUBE

PODCAST

Introduction of Ryuho Okawa's titles; topics ranging from self-help, current affairs, spirituality, religion, and the universe.